A Beautiful Place
on Yonge Street

Don Trembath

ORCA BOOK PUBLISHERS

Canadian Cataloguing in Publication Data

Trembath, Don, 1963 –
    A beautiful place on yonge street

    ISBN 1-55143-121-1

    I. Title.

Library of Congress Catalog Card Number: 98-85664

Orca Book Publishers gratefully acknowledges the support of our publishing programs provided by the following agencies: the Department of Canadian Heritage, the Canada Council for the Arts, and the British Columbia Arts Council.

Cover design by Christine Toller
Cover painting by Ljuba Levstek

Printed and bound in Canada

Orca Book Publishers
PO Box 5626, Station B
Victoria, BC V8R 6S4
Canada

Orca Book Publishers
PO Box 468
Custer, WA 98240-0468
USA

98 99 00   5 4 3 2 1

To Lisa

  The author would like to express his sincere thanks and acknowledgement for the generous funding support of The Alberta Foundation for the Arts, without which the writing of this novel would have been extremely difficult.

< 1 >

I met Sunny Taylor through her brother Mickey at a writing camp I went to in June. It was one of those week-long retreat deals. Mom and Dad sent me on it.

Mom said to me one day, just after school ended, "Harper, we have a surprise for you, and we think you're going to like it."

I looked at Herbie, my pet poodle, and we thought for a minute. Then I said, "How long will you be gone for?"

She didn't think that was particularly funny, even though I said it as a joke.

"We're sending you to a camp," she said, with this big smile on her face.

Now I don't know about you, but when somebody tells me they're sending me to a camp, I don't get very excited.

In the first place, I'm not too fussy about camps. I went to one once (sent by my parents, of course), and all I remember about it is sitting beside some kid, my partner, as he was called, who had a big bucket with him that he filled with leeches and snails and these little miniature fish. It was part of this "Nature World" project we had to do. My partner, his name was Michael, chose "Under The Sea."

He kept picking leeches from the bucket and saying to me, "Here, hold this one. It's cool. They clamp on to your skin and suck your blood. Then you have to use salt to get it off. Or sand. Or if you don't have any sand or salt nearby, you use fire. A lighter. Matches."

"No, thanks," I kept saying, figuring that if I wasn't at least polite with the kid, he might pour the bucket over my head.

"This one here, it feeds off garbage at the bottom of the lake. It can grow to be eighteen inches. Can you believe it? Eighteen inches."

"Amazing," I said, looking the other way.

"Could you imagine stepping out of a lake and having an eighteen-inch-long leech stuck to your leg?"

"No, I can't," I said, even though I could, and was, very easily.

"Man, that would be wild. You'd need a whole box of salt to get him off," he said, looking at the leech again. They were practically eye-to-eye. If leeches even have eyes, that is. "You wouldn't want to suck my blood, would you, little fella? No. Not my blood." Then he dropped the thing into the bucket and knocked me on the arm and said, "Enough of that. Come on. Let's go for a swim."

The other thing about going to camp is, I've never been too crazy about spending a whole bunch of time with people I don't even know. I mean, there's a lot of people I do know who I wouldn't want to spend time with, but it's even worse when you don't know them.

The only time I have ever had fun with people I don't know was when I joined a writing class a couple of years ago, but just because something happened once doesn't mean it's going to happen again and again and again. I don't think so, anyway.

"A camp?" I said to Mom, with some dejection. I thought she meant a real surprise, like a new computer, or news that my older brother William was moving to another part of the universe, like Toronto.

William doesn't live at home anymore. Neither does my sister, Clarissa. But man, he doesn't have to. He still gets under my skin.

Mom nodded. Her eyes were big, like marbles, and she still had a smile on her face, as if she had something more to say about it.

"A special youth camp," she said. "*For writers.*"

She put great emphasis on the "for writers" part.

I looked at her. Suddenly this sounded like a real surprise after all.

"A what?" I said. Herbie and I exchanged looks again. This time I was excited. He was suspicious.

"It's a camp for young writers," she said, pulling the brochure out of her pocket. She showed it to me. There were pictures of a lake and cabins and bunkhouses and this big rec room that had a kitchen and a fireplace in it. Then there were profiles of all the published writers who would be there and the names of all the sessions they would be teaching. It was nothing like the writing class I'd been in before, but it still looked pretty fun.

"We've registered you for one of the bunkhouses. There's a boys' and a girls'. We put you in the boys'. There's a little concession on the lake and a town nearby, but all your food and drink is paid for with the tuition, so you won't need much spending money."

"When is it?" I said.

"You leave Monday. We were very fortunate to get you in."

I looked at her when she said that, but I didn't say anything. What I think she meant by "fortunate" was that the writing camp people had said no to her the first time she called, probably because they were either full, or registration was over, but because answers like no do not sit well with Mom, she had to ask them again, and again, and maybe even again, before they finally got the message that she was not going to go away until they said yes.

That is one of the many ways that Mom operates. Dad says she's been able to run a very successful small business for many, many years with that attitude. I say, "Well, good for you, Mom. Careful you don't make any friends along the way," even though she has about a million of them.

She's not big or loud or anything. She's actually quite small — five foot three inches tall, one hundred and four pounds (she gives me these statistics every once in a while, as an example of how a person can stay fit and trim at any age). She's very neat and even if she's in the backyard pulling weeds or cleaning up the shed, her outfits are always well coordinated, and her clothes always go right into the washing machine when she goes inside.

Dad is a bit more of a slob when he's out in the yard. He wears clothes that Mom won't even *allow* in the washing machine, they're so dirty and greasy.

"Take them to the laundromat," she tells him. "They're not going in my machine."

The last time he ran for town council, he had me take some pictures of him with all this mud on his hands and face and clothes. He wanted to use them in his campaign pamphlets. He wanted to say something like, "Now *This* is Grassroots Politics!"

Mom talked him out of it, thank goodness.

He still won a seat, of course. Dad has been a town councillor for almost as long as he's been a medical doctor. He's also starting to lose his hair and has been on the "wrong side" (as Mom puts it) of two hundred pounds for over a year now, but we don't really talk about that too much.

Hair loss and weight gain are not exactly Dad's two favorite topics of conversation.

But anyway, back to the camp, I stopped sleeping on Saturday night, I was so excited. I didn't even bother going to bed on Sunday. I just sat up and watched TV and went through my bag for the hundredth time. By the time Monday morning came, I was looking like I needed to spend a week in the hospital, but I couldn't help it.

The idea of going somewhere and doing nothing but writing and talking and listening to writers for a whole week sounded perfect to me. You know why? Because first of all, as you may or may not know, I have become very interested in writing over the past couple of years, even to the point where I almost lost my head over something I wrote, but that's another story.

And second of all, because writing is the one thing that keeps me connected with my parents. Like whenever we're stuck for something to say to each other, which happens often, because we do not spend a lot of time together, one of us will bring up writing or reading as a topic for discussion, and we'll actually talk about it.

Mom and Dad will ask me questions about this or that and listen to my answer. Dad doesn't pretend to know everything and Mom says more than, "That's nice, honey," or "Good for you. Now pick up your dishes and rinse them in the sink before you take them to the dishwasher."

It's really quite enjoyable. I think Mom and Dad think so, too, and we don't think alike very often.

Anyway, on Monday morning, I said bye to Dad as he left for work and gave Herbie a big hug and a kiss, which practically makes Mom throw up, watching a human kiss a dog, and hopped in the car.

When I got to the camp, I checked in and was shown where to leave my stuff and which bed was mine in the bunkhouse. It was about three o'clock in the afternoon and I was suddenly feeling like I could curl up on the bed and be asleep in about five seconds, but then I remembered I had to go to my Orientation Session at the Rec Hall.

That's where I met Sunny's brother Mickey. He was this fairly tall, very skinny guy with short, dark hair and a perfectly round head. He was standing outside the hall reading a notice that had been posted on the wall next to the door. Everybody else was just walking right in, but he was standing there reading it, so I glanced at it as I walked by, in case it said something that I should know about.

"See this?" he said, pointing to the notice, after he saw me looking at it. He had a high-pitched voice and you could tell he was kind of nervous. Like maybe he was stalling before going inside.

"What is it?" I said. I hadn't had a chance to read it yet.

"It says, 'Welcome to Wilderness Writing Week. Make yourself at home. Don't forget to sign in for your Orientation Session.' Pretty nice, huh?"

I shrugged my shoulders. It seemed pretty normal to me, and there were welcome signs all over the place, so it wasn't like this one was any different.

"I think that's pretty nice," he went on, nodding his head. "'Welcome to Wilderness Writing Week.' I like that. Kind of a welcome, you know. It's nice to be welcomed like that."

I nodded and smiled a little.

"Yes, it is," I said.

"I think so, too," he said, turning towards me. "My name's Mickey, by the way. Mickey Taylor. This your first time here?"

"Yes," I said. "I'm Harper."

He just nodded and went on talking, as if he hadn't even heard me.

"Mine, too. I've never been here before. Driven by it a few times. I've been by here before. You know. On the road there. Drive by. Look around. Walk around. I've gotten out and walked around here before, right down there and around the cabins and that, but I've never actually been inside."

He had very big, brown eyes, like a squirrel's eyes, and it seemed like he was smiling almost the whole time he was talking, and constantly moving. He would put his hands in his pockets, then take them out. He pointed to the road. He showed me where he walked. He looked back at the sign.

He looked like he was probably about sixteen or so. The same age as me.

"You going in now?" I said. I thought I should ask, since I was going in, and I didn't want to just leave him there.

"Yeah, sure. May as well get it over with. After you. You go in first."

I walked in, feeling all of a sudden like his older brother, and found a place for us to sit.

A few minutes later, a woman walked to the front of the room and told us her name was Ms. Helen Dunsforth and that she would be taking us through this session. She had short black hair and glasses and was wearing blue jeans and this over-sized jean shirt that went about halfway down her legs.

I like it when people Mom's age dress like that – big shirts and old blue jeans and sandals. Mom is in her fifties. I would say that Ms. Dunsforth was about the same, but after that, I doubt if she and Mom would have too many other things in common.

For one thing, Ms. Dunsforth was not neat and trim. In fact, the clothes she was wearing looked like the kind of clothes Mom does her yardwork in.

For another, Ms. Dunsforth was here to talk with us about writing and books and creative expression and Mom is not really into all that. True, she talks with me about it, but she never actually does any writing herself, and the only books she knows about are ones by authors she sees profiled on television. Or cookbooks, but I don't know if they even count or not.

Anyway, there were about twenty of us in the room sitting on chairs. Three people sat on the floor. They sat cross-legged in a little circle at the front of the room, pretty well directly under the nose of Ms. Dunsforth, who didn't seem to mind.

The first thing she said was, "Well, everyone, welcome to Wilderness Writing Week."

I kind of rolled my eyes when she said it, as if to say, "Enough with the welcomes already," but I knew she was just being friendly.

Then Mickey gave a little shot with his elbow and smiled and nodded towards her and said, "They're pretty nice here, aren't they? Nice people here."

I think he was starting to feel comfortable, and very relieved. I don't know what he was expecting, but he didn't seem to be as nervous now as he had been a few minutes ago.

Ms. Dunsforth gave us the rundown on the place – when we would be in class and when we would have free time, the meal schedule and when the kitchen would be open for snacks, and finally, the rules.

"The number one rule for our camp is this," she said, taking off her glasses. She had them hanging on a little string around her neck. "When you are asked a question, any question, by a lecturer, or a guest author, or one of your peers, think before you answer. Don't just say, 'Oh, I don't know,' or 'Beats me,' or anything like that. Think. That is what we want you to do here. We want you to think and to get used to looking for the answers before you say you don't know them. When this week is over, we want your minds to be wide open to new ideas, new philosophies, new approaches to writing, and new approaches to thinking. And the biggest part of that is going to be getting used to using your mind to solve problems and answer questions before you throw in the towel with mind-numbing expressions like, 'I don't know. Beats me. Never seen it before. Never done this before.' Alright?"

Everybody was laughing when she finished. I think because everybody uses those expressions all the time. I know I do.

Then she said, "Okay. Now, the rest of the rules regarding the camp and so on are in your Orientation Kit. Read them over. Be sure you know them. And, if there are no further questions, let's get started."

She looked around at everybody, pointed her finger, and said, "You. What's your favorite color?"

She was pointing directly at me. I mean, I felt like she had a laser gun in her hand and she was boring a hole right through my chest.

I opened my mouth to say something, then I stopped. I couldn't say that. She had just spent the last ten minutes telling us not to say "I don't know," and that's exactly what I wanted to say, so I started telling myself, "Don't say 'I don't know.' Don't say 'I don't know.'"

"You want to say 'I don't know,' don't you?" she said.

Everybody around me laughed. Even I had to laugh, even though I wasn't sure if it was really all that funny.

So I nodded and started thinking about what my favorite color was.

All I could think about was fabric and patterns and materials.

Mom makes dresses for a living. Actually, she runs her own boutique, and she makes a lot more than just dresses, but she had been working on this one dress for about the past six months, and since it was for a woman who was about my size, I had been spending a lot of time in front of a mirror holding the thing under my chin as Mom tried to get the length right.

So I could think of no colors. Then all of a sudden, from beside me, Mickey said, "My sister likes yellow."

I don't know why he said it, if it was to rescue me or because he was absolutely bursting to say something or what, but he said it, and then Ms. Dunsforth said, "Good. We have a color. Yellow. Let's work with that." And the class went off talking about yellow, and about how yellow makes them feel, and what they think of when they see the color yellow, and what they think yellow tastes like.

It was all starting to get a little weird when Ms.

Dunsforth stopped the discussion and said, "What I want all of you to do is this. Tell me a story about yellow. It can be the history of yellow. The sound of yellow. The smell of yellow. Maybe you have something yellow at home that you want to tell us about. I want to hear your stories about yellow. Okay? Any questions?"

"Can I write a song?" said one of the three people sitting on the floor.

"Can you sing?" said Ms. Dunsforth.

"Not really."

"Then make it a short song. But yes. You can write a song, or a poem. No essays, please. This isn't English 101. I want to go the whole week without seeing a thesis statement or a conclusion or a topic sentence or anything else that has to do with essays."

"When do you want them?" said someone from the other side of the room.

"Tomorrow morning. Nine o'clock. Now, this isn't a do-or-die assignment. Please don't rush off to some library to look for reference materials. Use your heads. Write until you're done, then put your pens down and do something else. Have fun with it. And oh, yes. I also want you to pick a partner and interview each other. We'll have introductions in the morning as well."

Then she told us we could leave and enjoy the sunshine outside while it still lasted.

I walked out with Mickey. He was like a little kid, he was so excited.

"So, what do you think?" he said, when we got outside. "Pretty neat, isn't it? Writing about yellow.

I bet you've never done that before."

"I've come close," I said, thinking about some of the things I've written about at The Cafe.

"I haven't. Not about yellow. Blue I have. I've written about blue before. My neighbor, Samantha Brown, she had a rabbit named Bluebell that we wrote a story about. Bluebell the rabbit. I remember her. Small little thing. Fluffy. Big ears. Great big ears, you know."

I was thinking about the color yellow.

"Her favorite book was *Watership Down*."

I looked at him. I was going to say something like, "Your neighbor's rabbit liked *Watership Down*?" but I didn't. That drives me crazy when people do that. They hear you say something, and they know you've said it wrong, but instead of just letting it go, or saying, "You mean, your neighbor's favorite book was *Watership Down*? Not the rabbit's?" they get all excited and start cracking jokes like, "Hey, Mickey here knows a rabbit that reads books. Yeah, its favorite is *Watership Down*. Isn't that funny? He just said it. A rabbit that reads books." Ha, ha, ha.

"Samantha used to read Bluebell that story all the time," he said.

I looked at him again. This time I did say something.

"You mean your neighbor's rabbit's favorite book was *Watership Down*?"

"Uh-huh. She used to read it to her all the time. I used to sit on the balcony of our apartment and listen to her. Our balconies were almost touching.

They'd sit in one of those big lounge chairs. Samantha told me one time that that was the only book Bluebell ever sat still and listened to."

Now I was really glad I didn't say anything.

"Was there a Bluebell in that book?" I said, to change the subject, a little.

"I don't know. There was a Dandelion. I know that. And a Bigwig."

"I remember Bigwig."

"My mom liked Bigwig. That was her favorite."

"Your mom read *Watership Down*?" I said.

"It was her assignment," said Mickey, nodding. "She had to."

I looked at him.

"Her assignment?"

"She gave it to us."

"I don't get it."

"She asked us to read *Watership Down* and to write about it. We had to pretend we were rabbits. She wanted to know how we would have gotten along with all the other rabbits, and what we would have done when all the trouble came."

"So your mom's a teacher."

"No. She used to work for a dentist. Then she worked in a library. That's where she met my dad. Now she writes newsletters at home. We have a computer and a fax machine and everything. E-mail."

This was starting to get confusing.

"What was your dad doing in the library?"

"He works there. At the reference desk."

"Really?" I said. I had never met anyone whose dad worked at a library before. Most of the adults I know are doctors or lawyers or dentists. They're all friends of my parents.

"He's been there for about fourteen years now. Since Sunny and I were babies. Sunny's my sister."

"How old are you and Sunny?"

I don't usually ask people that question, but since I had just turned sixteen a couple of weeks before, I guess age was still on my mind.

"Sixteen," he said. "We're twins. She was born first. Then me. We turn seventeen this fall. In September."

I did a quick compute in my head. Mickey and his sister Sunny were about eight months older than me.

"Do you have any other brothers and sisters?" I said.

"Nope. That's it. Just me and Sunny and Mom and Dad."

"Where do you guys live?"

"The city. Edmonton. Downtown in an apartment. My dad walks to work."

Something else I was noticing about Mickey was, he talked in bullets. Little five- and six-word sentences at a time. Rat-a-tat. Rat-a-tat. The other thing was, his life was completely different from mine. His dad worked in a library. He had a twin sister. They lived downtown.

"Where do you guys go to school?" I said.

"We home school," said Mickey. "That's what I was telling you about before."

This one was the capper.

"You go to school at home?"

"Uh-huh."

"Who are your teachers? Your mom and dad?"

"Pretty well. We have a neighbor who's an artist. She gives us art lessons. Sunny goes to the Art Gallery, too. And we go to the pool for swimming. My dad has a friend who's a mechanic. We're going to start seeing him about taking apart engines and stuff like that. Learning about cars and everything. Brakes. The oil. How to check the oil."

We walked in silence for a few minutes after that. I wasn't sure where we were going, since I couldn't remember how we got from the Rec Hall back to the bunkhouses. But I really wasn't too worried about it.

I figured I had already done my interview of Mickey, with all those questions I had asked him. I hadn't meant to, really. I was just very interested in practically everything he was saying. Even the writing assignment his mom had given him. "Pretend you're a rabbit. How would you have gotten along with the other rabbits?" That's a pretty good topic, if you ask me. I think I could have had a lot of fun with something like that.

"So," said Mickey, after a minute or so. "You want to come back to our cabin for a while? Maybe we could work together on some of this stuff. The interviews and that."

"You mean the bunkhouse?" I said.

"No. We're staying in a cabin. My dad and sister came with me. Mom stayed home. She might come up at the end of the week. She might come up here. My dad and sister are here with me now. My dad's on vacation. We went to Hawaii last Christmas, so this is all the holiday time he gets. He figured he might as well come here with me rather than pay for me to come here and then pay for all of us to go somewhere else. All he does is read books anyway. You know. That's about all he does. Chops wood and reads his books. Sunny came so my mom could be alone. She wanted to be alone, so Sunny came here. She's on vacation with my dad. They're just here to relax, look around. Read some books."

Mickey had this habit of repeating himself all the time.

"Sure," I said, with a shrug. "I guess so."

We walked on a little bit more down this path through the bush, then we turned a corner that led to a little clearing, and in the clearing were a couple of cabins. One looked like it was empty. In front of the other one, just off the front porch, there was a man sitting in a lawn chair reading a book. He had a fire going in the fire pit in front of him and there was all of this chopped wood in a heap next to him. Behind him was a big thick log with an axe in it.

The man was about ninety percent bald, with a few little wisps of hair sticking out over his ears and on top of his head. He wore wire-framed glasses. He looked like he was pretty tall, and fairly thin. He had no shirt on and was wearing shorts and sandals. On the ground beside him was a can of Coke.

"Hello, Mick," the man said, as we approached. "How's the novel?"

"Oh, no novels yet," said Mickey. "We don't do those until tomorrow." Then he said, "Dad, this is

Harper. He's a friend of mine from class."

"Hi, Mr. Taylor," I said, and shook his hand, which I'm still not very good at, even though Dad gives me hand-shaking lessons at least five times a week.

"You can lose a person's vote with a handshake," he likes to say, squeezing my hand until my knees bend.

"Nice to meet you, Harper," said Mr. Taylor. "That wouldn't be after Harper Lee, would it? *To Kill A Mockingbird*. One of the best books ever written."

"I don't think so," I said. I had never heard of Harper Lee before. The name of the book sounded familiar, though.

"Your parents did you a favor if it is,'" he said. "They could have named you Atticus. Or Calpurnia, if you'd been a girl."

"Where's Sunny?" said Mickey.

"She took her bike to the pay phone," said his dad. "She's trying to order Kentucky Fried Chicken from somewhere." Then he rolled his eyes and shook his head.

"Oh, boy," said Mickey, with a smile, rubbing his hands together. "I hope she gets some."

"Oh, she'll get some," said his dad, looking back at his book. "If she has to call down to Kentucky, she'll get some."

"We haven't had that in about a week now," said Mickey. "I'll bet it's been a full week since we had some of that." Then he looked at me and said, "You like Kentucky Fried Chicken?"

I shrugged my shoulders.

"Sure," I said. "I don't have it very often."

Mom is not exactly a spokesperson for fast foods. Even when we go to McDonald's, she's after me to buy a fat-free muffin or a salad, which are really not the kinds of things I go for at a place like that.

"You want to stay for supper?" said Mickey.

I shrugged my shoulders again and nodded. I mean, I wasn't dying for him to ask me over or anything, but it sounded fun, having chicken in a cabin, or around the fire, and I was sure that if I brushed my teeth four times a day from now until the end of camp, Mom wouldn't smell any of it on my breath.

Mickey turned to his dad and said, "Is that okay, if Harper stays over?"

"It's okay with me," said Mr. Taylor.

"We have to work on an assignment later. We have a little homework to do."

I had forgotten about that.

Then from behind me I heard a bell, and I turned around and saw a girl riding up to the cabin on her bike. She was wearing faded blue overalls and a white t-shirt underneath. She was about as tall as Mickey and just as thin, and she had the smoothest, whitest skin I had ever seen. Even from that first glimpse of her, I could that see her skin was smooth.

I have no idea why I noticed that right away.

She got off her bike and looked at me and smiled. She had long, straight, dark hair and Mickey's big, brown eyes. But on her, they looked even deeper and darker.

I felt like I could stare at them forever.

"Fifty dollars," she said. Her voice was a little high, and sweet.

I think I liked her from the second I saw her, in case you couldn't tell.

At first I thought she was talking to me, like maybe she was telling me how much her bike cost or something. But then I realized she was talking to her dad, telling him how much the chicken was.

Her dad said he had never spent fifty dollars on chicken before and she said that about half of that was for delivery. Then she went inside the cabin.

When she came out again, she was wearing glasses.

"My contacts were driving me nuts," she said, to no one in particular.

"Sunny," said Mickey. "This is my friend Harper. I met him in my writing class."

"Oh," she said. She smiled and walked towards me and stuck out her hand, so I did the same with mine. Her hand was small and cool and soft. "Nice to meet you, Harper."

"Nice to meet you," I said.

We made eye contact for about a second.

"How long is this chicken going to take to get here?" said Mr. Taylor.

"About half an hour," said Sunny. "They have to cook it, then find somebody who can drive it up."

Her dad looked at his watch, then picked up his book from his lap and asked Mickey if he could get him another Coke from inside. Mickey went off, and I was standing there with Sunny.

I was going to say something, although I wasn't

sure exactly what, when she turned to her dad and said, "So, Dad, there's a whole bunch of trails around here we can take tomorrow. There's one that goes right down to the lake."

Her dad nodded, but didn't lift his eyes from his book.

Everything was pretty quiet after that until, from out of nowhere, my mouth blurted out, "I hear you like yellow."

Both Sunny and her dad looked at me. I guess they weren't sure who I was talking to. That, or they thought it was kind of a weird thing to say, which it was, when you think about it, especially to people who are practically complete strangers.

"Mickey told me," I said, by way of an elaboration, which didn't seem to help.

"Mickey told you I like yellow?" said Sunny.

I gave her the full story.

"Our teacher asked me what color I liked, and I couldn't think of anything because my mom's a dressmaker, and all I could think about was this dress she's been making me wear for the past year, so Mickey bailed me out and said you liked yellow."

I was very nervous, talking to her like that.

Sunny was quiet for a moment or two, as if she was thinking, or planning her escape. Then she said, "Yellow is the one color I *don't* like. Everyone used to buy me yellow things when I was little. Pants, shirts, pajamas, booties. I guess they thought with a name like Sunny, I should always look like the sun. I look in old photo albums and it's like the only color I ever wore. Yellow this. Yellow that. Dark yellow. Light yellow. Yellow polka dots. Yellow stripes. There's one picture of me where I'm wearing a yellow snowsuit, yellow mittens, a yellow scarf and a yellow hat. I looked like a big frozen banana."

She wasn't looking at me when she said this. She was staring off in the distance somewhere. Then she turned and looked right at me and said, "Your mother has been making you wear what?"

"A dress," I said, really wishing that I hadn't opened my mouth at all, much less to say what I had said.

"That's what I thought."

"I'm not really wearing it. I just hold it up so my mom can check the length. It's too skinny for me to actually put on. I've tried several times." That last part was a joke.

She didn't laugh. She just nodded her head slowly, as if she was considering whether she should believe me or not. Then she said, "So, what else did you guys do?"

I shrugged my shoulders.

"We talked about how to think. The rules. The kind of writing we'll be doing."

"What kind is that?"

"Well, for tomorrow we have to write a story about yellow, and interview our partner for introductions."

"What kind of a story about yellow are you going to write?"

"I'm not sure," I said, but all of a sudden an idea had come into my head. It had nothing to do with Sunny, but everything to do with a little kid who wore a yellow shirt. It was a true story, too. I couldn't wait to write it.

"Well, don't write about me, thank you very much. I hate yellow."

We didn't say anything after that. I didn't think I should tell her that I had just had this magnificent brainstorm of an idea that had absolutely nothing to do with her. I did want to thank Mickey for coming up with the color, though. It was perfect.

A few minutes later, Sunny said, "Well, I'm going for a walk."

She wasn't looking at her dad or me when she said it. She just said it and started walking towards the road she had gone for her bike ride on.

I just stood there, even though I kind of felt like going with her. Actually, I really felt like going with her, but it would have felt funny just heading off on a walk with someone I had just met, especially with her dad sitting right there.

"You want to come?" she said, turning around and looking at me.

She caught me off guard. Then Mickey came out of the cabin with a can of Coke in his hand and she asked him if he wanted to go. He said no. He wanted to sit and read for a while.

Then she looked back at me.

"I'm just going to wait for the chicken," she said.

"Sure," I said, and off we went.

It was the first time I had ever gone for a walk alone with a girl in my entire life.

< 2 >

Our trip down the road turned out to be quite the little outing, I tell you.

Sunny took the longest strides I have ever seen a girl take on a walk to wait for chicken. She was practically at the end of the road before I caught up with her. She had her arms swinging by her sides and the whole bit.

"What's the rush?" I said. I was almost out of breath.

"Who's rushing?" she said, marching along.

"I was kind of hoping you were," I said, still scrambling to keep up. I don't go for walks very often, and I had never walked this fast in my life, not even when my poodle, Herbie, was running away from a cat.

"My mom and I go for a walk like this every morning. It's very invigorating. We go through the park or right downtown. Sometimes we stop for coffee on the way home. Or pick up some bagels and the newspaper. Or a magazine."

"How do you drink coffee walking like this?" I was practically running to keep up with her.

She turned and looked at me.

"We wait until we get it home. It's still hot when we get there."

We marched on, our feet crunching on the gravel beneath us. There were a few other people out and about, mostly on bikes or poking along some of the pathways that broke off from the road.

After another five minutes or so we rounded a bend that came to an end at the paved road that winds in from the highway to the camp. At the corner was a phone booth and another sign saying, "Welcome." Besides that, there was nothing.

Sunny came to a stop and looked around in all directions, even the direction we had just come from, and took a deep breath and said, "Not here yet, I guess."

I looked around as well. There was definitely no sign that anyone carrying fifty dollars' worth of Kentucky Fried Chicken had been here, not that I knew what that sign would be, aside from a big bucket of chicken, or a guy standing right here in front of us, wearing a red and white striped uniform and a little hat on his head.

Sunny kept moving around, walking into the middle of the highway to look down the road to see if anyone was coming, swinging her arms around, throwing a few stones. I figured she was either very hungry or not completely comfortable with having me around, even though she had invited me to come along.

Then all of a sudden she stopped moving, let her hands drop by her sides, tilted her head towards the sky, closed her eyes, and let out this big sigh. Then she opened her eyes and looked at me and said, "I'm feeling stress."

I looked at her and said nothing.

"Can't you tell?" she said, still looking at me.

"Not really," I said. How could I know if she was feeling stress or not? I had only known her for about fifteen minutes.

She closed her eyes again and took a deep breath. Then she started talking.

"Right now, my mom is at home, fanatically cleaning every square inch of everything because my aunt came over for a visit last week and she always leaves my mom completely stressed out. I have another aunt who is probably down to about two weeks to live. The last time I saw her she had three weeks. But they told her four months ago that she had seven days, so what do they know. And, I forgot my drawing board at home, so I can't do any drawing."

She looked at me with a look of complete sadness and frustration.

"All I can do here is go for walks, ride my bike, read books, and eat chicken."

"That sounds okay," I said. I didn't know what else to say, or even if I should say anything at all.

"I know that," said Sunny. "I know it's okay. I'm not complaining. But there are times in my life when I want more than 'okay,' and this is one of them. In fact, I don't ever want to settle for just 'okay,' and if I had just remembered my stupid drawing board, this week would have been perfect. I had it by the door and everything. I don't know how I forgot it."

We were quiet for a minute, then I said, "What do you draw?"

Sunny closed her eyes and took another deep breath and let it out. Then she opened her eyes and smiled at me.

"Landscapes, mostly. Sketches. People. Feelings. I'm an artist."

"Are you?" I said. I had never met a real artist before.

"Well, not really. Not yet. But if you say you're something, you have a much better chance of actually becoming it than if you don't. It gets your mind there first. Everything else just follows along."

I didn't say anything. I had to think about that for a second.

Then I said, "So, what's this about your aunt?"

"Which one?" said Sunny.

"Either one," I said. I mean, I didn't want to pry, but it sure seemed to me that she felt like talking, and it sounded like she had some pretty interesting stories to tell.

"Well, my Auntie Babs comes and visits from Toronto about once every five years, and this was the fifth year, so she came, and she did what she always does, which is criticize everything my mom does, and everything we're doing, and every time she leaves, my mom has to spend about a week by herself cleaning the apartment."

"I don't get it," I said. My mom spends every week cleaning the house, and if I ever had my say about it, she would always do it by herself.

"It's her way of getting over the visit. It relieves her anxiety. Plus, it gets rid of Auntie Babs. She cleans inside the cupboards, the door handles, picture frames, windows. If Auntie Babs looked through a window in our apartment, Mom cleans it when she leaves."

"What kinds of things does she say?"

"Oh, you know. 'How's the *newsletter* business?' 'Written any good *articles* lately?' 'Gotten any *pay* for anything you write yet?' She knows my mom has always wanted to write books. And she's always asking me when I'm going to come out to Toronto to meet some *real* artists. I took her to my drawing class at the Art Gallery, and all she did was talk about how small it was and how she didn't recognize anyone. Finally I said to her, 'Well, no one's recognizing you either, Auntie Babs.' She fancies herself to be quite the high-society woman."

"What does she do in Toronto?"

"She runs a bakery."

"A bakery?"

"Yes. Isn't that funny? She's this tall, skinny woman. She looks just like my dad, if you could imagine him with hair, and eyeliner, and she's up at, like, three o'clock every morning to open her bakery, and she goes to bed at about seven every night, and she carries on like she's Mrs. Hollywood whenever she comes out here."

"How does she ever see anything?"

"She stays up late on weekends. She actually has a beautiful place. It's right on Yonge Street. You go in there at seven o'clock in the morning and it's like a garden of bread. You just stand in the doorway and close your eyes and smell. She wants me to come stay with her in the fall. She says there's an art school that's the best in the country, and she can get me in. She knows the director. She sells him bagels every morning, or something. I can just take my grade twelve from there. Mom can E-mail my assignments to me. Or fax them."

"Are you?" I said. I knew it wasn't any of my business, but I pretty well had to ask.

"I doubt it. Not if my parents are still alive."

"Would they let you go if you wanted to?"

"I don't know," she said, looking down the road for the chicken. "Probably. I keep going back and forth on it. I'll have to see. It's really a beautiful place she has down there. And I know it would be good for me, to go down and paint and study art."

"What about your other aunt?" I said. I wanted to change the topic.

Sunny looked down the road for another minute, then she said, "Well, my Auntie Babs is my least favorite aunt and my Auntie Mavis is my favorite."

Then she went quiet again.

"And my Auntie Mavis is dying of cancer."

We were both quiet after that.

"When they first found out what she had, they gave her a week to live. Then they put her on some kind of treatment and gave her a couple of months. Now she's going downhill again, so no one knows how long she has."

"A *week*?" I said. I couldn't imagine anyone being told they have one week to live.

Sunny nodded.

"They told her she has a week to live. She told them, 'Fine. I'm going home.' Well, she didn't say fine. I'm sure she was in shock at the time. But she wanted to get home to be with her pets. She has two dogs and two cats. She wanted to be the one to tell them she was going away."

Sunny's voice started to crack and I could see her chin and lips starting to tremble.

"So she went home and told her pets. Then she phoned my mom. They're sisters. My mom went over there and found Auntie Mavis on the couch with all four dogs and cats beside her. They had never sat together like that ever. The two cats don't get along very well."

"Where is she now?" I said.

"She's at home. We're having a birthday party for her next month. Tentatively scheduled, of course. My dad says we should have a party for her whether she's there or not, but we'll see."

"How old is she?"

"She'll be sixty. Old enough to collect her pension, she likes to say. She's pretty funny, actually. She's the one who got me into drawing. I used to love visiting with her. I still do, but she gets really tired and sometimes she doesn't remember what we're talking about. She can barely see anymore."

I could not imagine visiting with someone who had one week to live. Or a month. Or even a year.

"Mickey reads to her a lot. I show her my pictures."

She was looking down the road again when she was talking. Then, suddenly, she said, "I bet this is it," and pointed to a car coming our way.

She was right. A kid drove up in a little black wreck of a car that made more noise than a flock of chickens heading to the Colonel's house, and rolled down his window and handed us about five bags of chicken and french fries and the biggest tub of gravy I've ever seen in my life. You could wash it out and put it on your head and use it as a rain hat, it was so big.

"You bring ketchup?" said Sunny, leaning towards the car. I guess she was finished talking about her aunts.

"In the bag," said the kid, who barely turned his head to talk to her.

He was a fat, pouty-looking kid with a ball cap on backwards and a toothpick in his mouth. He was probably around eighteen or nineteen. He looked totally bored to be here.

Sunny looked through all the bags until she found the one with the ketchup in it.

"Salt?"

"Uh-huh."

"Vinegar?"

The kid thought for a second and looked at Sunny.

"I don't think there's vinegar," he said. "You didn't ask for vinegar."

"I always ask for vinegar," said Sunny, looking right at him. "I've asked for vinegar since I was seven years old. Why wouldn't I ask for it now?"

"Well, there's no vinegar," said the kid.

"Well, there goes some of your tip," said Sunny. She took a dollar out of her hand and put it in her pocket. "They always forget the vinegar," she added, looking at me.

The kid watched her, then he reached over in his car, opened his glove box, rummaged around for about five minutes, and pulled a couple of very old packets of vinegar out and handed them to her.

She looked at them.

"How old are these?" she said.

"Six months last week," said the kid.

Sunny gave him a look. Then she dug the dollar out of her pocket and gave it to him.

"Any napkins?" she said, peering into one of the bags.

The kid rolled his eyes and looked at me. I didn't say anything. I didn't know whose side to take on this one. It drives me crazy when Mom checks everything and asks a whole bunch of questions whenever we have takeout. When we order Chinese food, she'll take every container out of every bag and open the lid to make sure the shrimp and black bean sauce has enough black bean sauce on it, and the beef and greens isn't all greens and no beef, even though she hardly ever eats the beef. Then she'll do the old check for soya sauce and plum sauce and do a count of all the fortune cookies to make sure everyone gets one.

"What kind of good fortune can you hope to have if everyone gets a cookie but you?" she said the last time she did it.

"What kind of good fortune can you hope to have if you believe what's written inside a wooden little cookie you can't even eat?" I said back.

"There's napkins," said the kid. Then he put his car in gear and started to creep very slowly away from Sunny, who was still looking in one of the bags.

"How about those little washcloth thingies? Did you throw some of those in?"

The kid turned his car around.

"They're in there," he said, through the passenger window.

"How many?" said Sunny.

"Thirty-five," said the kid. Then he waved and zipped off down the road.

"I don't even see them," said Sunny, who didn't even look when the kid drove away.

"He said they're in there," I said, as if to imply that of all the people in the world who may tell a lie from time to time, a Kentucky Fried Chicken delivery boy stuck on the side of a highway while some fanatic goes through every bag he's just dropped off wasn't one of them.

"Well, I guess we can always just wash our hands," said Sunny, looking at me and smiling. She seemed to be in much better spirits than when she was telling me about her aunts. "Come on. Let's go."

We walked back up the road towards her cabin.

"So, tell me about your family," she said, as we were walking.

I rolled my eyes. Just when I was starting to work up an appetite, she had to ask me about that.

< 3 >

I wrote my story about the color yellow the next morning. I woke up early, very early, actually, when the guy sleeping in the bed beside me got up to go to the bathroom, and stubbed his toe on the gigantic woodbox we have in the middle of our bunkhouse. He spent the next five minutes hopping around on one leg cursing and screaming to himself. Then he lost his balance and fell on top of me.

Not exactly my preferred way of waking up in the morning.

I tried going back to sleep, but I couldn't, partially because my heartbeat was up to about fifteen thousand beats per second, but also because the only thing I thought about all night was writing this story and reading it to Sunny.

I don't know why I was thinking that. It's not like she had asked to hear it or anything. I guess I just thought it would be nice to read to someone different for a change. Plus, I liked the idea of spending more time with her.

Mickey and I had talked about our stories after we'd polished off half the chicken and about a third of the fries Sunny had ordered. The salad had just sat there until Mr. Taylor, who had eaten as many fries as any of us, and hadn't looked at the salad either, said, "Come on, you guys. Eat some of this." Then we all had some, including him.

We ate outside on the little table on the deck that was attached to their cabin.

About halfway through the meal, Mickey said, "Hey, let's play Twenty Questions." Sunny got all excited and said, "I'll go first. I'll go first."

Twenty Questions, I was told, since I had never heard of it before, was this game where one person picks either a person, place, thing, animal, vegetable, or mineral, and the rest of the people have to guess who or what it is. You can only ask questions that can be answered with yes or no.

"Colonel Sanders," said her dad, to start the game.

Sunny gave him a look.

"No."

"A chicken," said Mickey.

"No."

It was my turn. I didn't have a clue what to ask. I didn't even know what we were looking for.

"Is it a person?" I said.

"Yes," said Sunny, and she smiled. I guess the hunt was on.

We went in regular order after that.

"Is this person a male?" said her dad.

"Yes."

"Is he alive?" said Mickey.

"No."

"Was he an artist or a performer of some kind?" I said. I was starting to get into it now.

Sunny made a face. She was thinking. "Hmmm," she said.

"Was he a writer?" said her dad, out of turn, but I didn't mind.

"Yes."

Then there was a pause. Mickey was deep in thought. He stared at Sunny. She stared back at him. He was trying to think, and she was trying to distract him.

No one touched their food.

"What books has she read lately?" said their dad, interrupting Mickey's thoughts.

"I'm not sure," said Mickey. Then he said, "Hang on for a second. I have to use the bathroom."

Sunny eyed him as he stood to leave the table, then she jumped up as he was about to step into the cabin.

"No going in my book bag," she said. "You stay right here until the game is over."

"What book bag?" said Mickey, looking offended. "I'm going to the bathroom."

"You are not," said Sunny. "You're going to look at my books."

Mickey stared at her for a second, then decided to forget it and returned to the table.

"All right," he said, with resignation and a little smile.

"Was worth a try," said her dad.

"Going to the bathroom," said Sunny, shaking her head. "You just went to the bathroom. You went in right after me. The least you could have done is said you're getting some pop. Then I would have believed you."

"I'll remember that," said Mickey.

Then we got back to our game.

"Does he write books for kids?" said her dad.

"Yes. And adults," said Sunny. "I had to add that in."

"Was it one of the books we read for school?" said Mickey.

"Yes."

"Was it a detective story?" I said, hoping she would say yes, so I could call upon my vast and hopefully superior knowledge of detective novels that I have read, thanks to my brother, who left his massive collection at home when he moved out.

"No," said Sunny.

About five minutes and another batch of questions later, her dad snapped his fingers and said, "*The Little Prince,* Saint-Exupery."

Sunny nodded and smiled.

"Got it," she said. "Twenty-five guesses to get that." Then she looked at me and said, "If you ever want to read a good book, read that one."

Mickey went next. His mystery person, or whatever you want to call it, was Roger Clemens of the Toronto Blue Jays.

I guess Mickey's a baseball nut. Sunny said, "You could have picked someone harder than that" after she got it, and he went down almost the entire

Blue Jays order, just to see if she recognized the names or not.

She said no to most of them.

"Wait 'til they win the World Series again. Then you'll know them all again," said Mickey. "You'll know who they are."

"Wait 'til I move to Toronto," said Sunny. Her dad gave her a look. She looked at Mickey and winked. He didn't wink back.

Then their dad went. He picked Bill Gates, the guy who owns everything that has anything to do with computers.

I was the one who figured it out first, mainly because my parents and I had gotten into this big discussion about computers just before I left for this camp. Dad wanted to get me a new one. Mom said that the one we had was just fine.

"It's the way of the future," said Dad. "Instead of employers asking, 'Do you have your own car?' the way they did twenty years ago, they'll be saying, 'Do you have your own laptop? Laser printer? How long did it take you to learn Windows?'"

Mom rolled her eyes.

"Every time I see a new computer, I think of that little man who owns all of them. What's his name?"

"William Gates," said Dad. "One of the wealthiest men in the world. If not *the* wealthiest. His friends call him Bill. And everyone who owns a computer is his friend."

"That's not true," said Mom.

"No," said Dad. "But it should be."

That ended their conversation. I don't think that

last bit did me any favors in terms of getting a new computer either, but we'll have to see.

Anyway, after I guessed Bill Gates, it was my turn. I decided to get tricky and picked Richard Adams, the guy who wrote *Watership Down*, the book Mickey and I had talked about. The one with all the rabbits.

It took them four guesses to get it.

"We're good," said Sunny, as if she was stating a fact.

"We're professionals," said Mickey, nodding his head.

We were about to go around the table again when Mr. Taylor said, "I have to get that fire going again. Count me out." Then Sunny decided she was going to have a shower. So Mickey and I finished off our interviews and talked about the next day of class. He was pretty excited about this story about yellow business.

"I was thinking about writing about the sun," he said. "You know, the sun? How it keeps us warm and does so many things. How it helps plants grow and burns our backs. I was thinking about doing something like that. I did a paper on the sun once."

I didn't tell him what I was writing about. It wasn't like I was keeping a secret or anything, or that I thought he was going to say, 'Hey, I'm gonna write about that, too. That's a great idea!'

I just didn't feel like telling anybody quite yet.

"The sun is a good idea," I said, nodding. It was a pretty good idea, after I thought about it.

"I think I'm going to write about that," said Mickey.

A few minutes later, I said goodbye and started to leave for my bunkhouse. Mickey waved and said, "Okay, well, it's nice meeting you, Harper."

I turned and looked at him.

"I'm coming back, you know. In the morning."

"I know that," said Mickey. "I'm just telling you that now. Why wait until the end of the trip? It's nice meeting you. I'm glad I met you. Have a good sleep."

I knew what I wanted to write about when I got up in the morning, so it wasn't a real big deal doing it. The Rec Hall was open all day and night, so I just went down there with a pen and my writing pad.

There was no one else around when I got there. After about half an hour, the woman who runs the kitchen came in and plugged in the coffeemaker. She was short and kind of heavy and had hands like a carpenter. Her fingers were thick and strong. She looked like she could pop the lid off any jar in the world, her hands were so strong.

About fifteen minutes after she arrived, she asked me if I wanted a cup of coffee. I said, "No thanks." Then she asked me what I took in it and I said, "Nothing, thanks," and shook my head, so she gave me a cup of black coffee and a cookie.

"Don't tell anyone about the cookie," she said.

"You always up this early?" I said. I didn't really mind getting a cup of coffee. I had to start drinking the stuff sometime. Besides, I was in such a good mood. My story was going really well and, to top it off, I was feeling like a real writer.

I started feeling like that when I was walking down the path towards the hall. I felt like one of those people you see profiled on t.v. all the time. They're always walking along the ocean or down a mountain trail or along some gravel road to the little hut or chalet or garden house that they write in.

There's always this voice in the background saying things like, "When he was seventeen, Harry Hopkins began writing stories and sending them off to magazines across the country. By the time he was twenty-five, he had written four books, three of them award-winners. Today, at sixty, he is regarded as one of the finest fiction writers in the world. Here at his home on Gula-Gula Island off the coast of British Columbia, he talks about his life and his career."

For me, they would be saying something like, "When he was sixteen, Winslow was welcomed into the prestigious Wilderness Writing Camp, and it was there that he penned his first and perhaps most famous piece of work, 'The Happy Shirt: A Story About The Color Yellow.' He tells us now how the story came about."

"Yes, yes, of course I remember it. I was just a boy at the time. On the brink of falling in love, as I recall …"

The woman who ran the kitchen looked at me.

"You don't like the cookie?" she said.

I looked down at my cookie. I hadn't even touched it.

"No, no. I said, Are you always up this early?" I said each word a little bit slower and more carefully, in case she couldn't hear very well, which was beginning to seem like a very strong possibility.

She smiled.

"You eat that one. Then I'll get you another one. Okay?"

Then she patted me on the arm and went back into the kitchen.

I ate the cookie and went back to my writing.

About half an hour later, I finished my story and got up from my chair and yawned and stretched and walked around to try and find a clock.

There were a few more people around. I recognized a couple of them from my class the day before. They were all going to the showers or popping into the Rec Hall for a cup of coffee. I said hi to them and a couple of them said hi back. I was feeling pretty chipper at the moment.

One guy, who had his hair in a ponytail and the beginnings of a very scruffy beard growing on his face, was walking around with a book by someone named Walt Whitman pressed up to his nose. He started reading out loud as he approached me. "Good morning, my friend!" he said, lowering the book from his face. "Have you sang a song this morning?"

I wasn't feeling that chipper.

"No, I haven't," I said.

"Then sing one now," he said, marching on. I could hear him beginning to sing a song of his own. "Oh, when the saints. Oh, when the saints. Oh, when the saints come marching in …!"

I asked a girl for the time, and she pushed up her sleeve and checked her watch and said it was six-thirty. "But I'm not sure if that's New York time or here," she added. She was wearing an over-sized jean jacket and sweat pants and sandals. She had a red beret on her head.

"New York time?" I said.

"Yes. That's what I like to think about when I'm writing. The City of New York. Living in a loft somewhere. Walking my dogs down the street late at night. Hanging out at the Village."

"The Village?"

"You wouldn't know it. I think that's the time here. I haven't changed my watch yet. But don't ask me tomorrow. You'll be two hours early for every-thing."

I walked back up to the bunkhouse and picked up my towel, soap, toothpaste, and toothbrush. I shaved at Christmas, so I didn't even bother bring-ing a razor or shaving cream with me. That was Dad's big joke. He told everyone we saw over the holidays that I had shaved for the first time in my life, and that I would do it again next Christmas whether I needed to or not.

I went over my story again on the way to the showers. I always do that. I write something down and then I think about it and think about it.

My story was about this little kid who used to live beside us. He was about eight years old when he moved away, so he was probably around five when this story took place.

I was outside doing nothing in the backyard one

day when I heard him crying next door. I went and looked over our fence, and he was just sitting there, cross-legged, in the middle of the yard, in his little shorts and a blue t-shirt, with his chin in his hands.

I said, "Hey, Henry, what's the matter?"

His name was Henry. Can you believe that? I thought Harper was bad.

"My happy shirt's in the washing machine and mommy says I can't take it out."

He said it so quietly I had to ask him about five times before I finally heard what he said.

"Your 'happy shirt?'" I said. I needed to clarify.

He nodded.

"What's a 'happy shirt?'"

"It's a shirt that makes me happy."

"What color is it?"

"Lellow."

That's how he always said yellow. "Lellow."

"Why does yellow make you happy?"

He looked at me and said, "Well, if you have any treats at your house, I'll tell you."

I loved the way that kid talked. He could be so direct and he spoke his mind so clearly.

I went inside and grabbed a couple of Oreos and came back out and gave him one.

"So?" I said, as he demolished his cookie. "Why does yellow make you happy?"

"Well," he said, finishing his last bite. "Do you have anything to drink?"

I gave him a look, then I went inside again and looked around. We had apple juice, but I didn't think that would be enough to get him to talk. We had pop, but that would only lead to more trouble if his mom found out. Or worse, if mine did. So, I settled on making him some cherry Kool-Aid and dropping an ice cube in it.

I took his drink outside and gave it to him.

He took about four big gulps, then lowered the glass from his mouth, leaving the biggest cherry-red mustache above his lip that I think I've ever seen.

"You know, half that drink is still on your face," I said.

He ran his tongue around his mouth.

"So, now are you going to tell me?"

"Uh-huh," he said, nodding. "I call it my happy shirt because when I was little, that's what my grandma called it."

"Your grandma?"

"Yes. That's what I said. My grandma."

"Your grandma said yellow was a happy color?"

"Yes."

"And that's all there is to it?"

"Except one more thing." He held up one little finger.

"What's that?"

"Another cookie."

I laughed. I always laughed when I talked with Henry. He was such a sweet kid. Then I said, "What is this about when you were little? How old were you when you were little?"

"Uhhm," he said, scrunching his face. He was quite the little problem-solver, as I recall. "I was eleben."

"Eleven?"

"Yes. That's what I said. Eleben."

"Isn't eleven higher than five?"

He shook his head.

"I think it is."

"Well," he said, "maybe it is for some people, but not for me."

The next day, I was in the backyard again, and he was sitting at his little plastic picnic table in his own backyard drawing a picture. He was singing and humming and talking to himself and using every color of crayon and marker he had in his bucket.

"Hey, Henry," I said. "How are you feeling to-day?"

He stood up and climbed on top of his table and stuck his little sparrow chest out and said, "See this? This is my happy shirt."

And sure enough, it was bright yellow, and it had certainly made him happy.

I wrote my story in the exact way I remembered everything happening. And then at the end I wrote, "I think I'll have to get one of those happy shirts for myself one day. I could use one sometimes. I think we all could."

I was pretty pleased with it. It wasn't deep or anything, but I thought it was okay. Besides, I knew it was real, and if there is one thing I've learned about writing, it's that it has to be real. Not phony or trumped up to be funny or anything. That's some-thing my writing teacher, his name is Josh, used to tell me. A story doesn't have to be true necessarily, but once you start adding things just to make it funny, or sad, then you're cheating it. And if you're cheating your story, you're cheating yourself.

I'm not completely sure what all that means, except for when I'm telling a story about Henry and his yellow shirt, I'm not supposed to add anything to it. So, I didn't.

I stopped by the Taylors' cabin after my shower and Mickey was just waking up. He asked me to come back in about half an hour so we could go to class together. Then he said, "Or, you could just stay here. I'm putting some coffee on for my dad. My dad likes coffee in the morning. You could have some with him."

All of a sudden I was becoming Mr. Coffee Drinker.

I was about to say no thanks when one of the bedroom doors creaked open and Sunny stepped out. Actually, she staggered out, wearing one of those extra-long t-shirts for pajamas, this one with a giant picture of Big Bird from "Sesame Street" on it. She looked even thinner in it than she had in her overalls last night. She didn't look sick or anything. She just seemed to be naturally thin, or, as Mom would put it, she was "one of the lucky ones."

Her hair was all messed around and she didn't have her glasses on. She put her hand out to the wall for support and started walking towards me. Then she stuck her hand in my face and said, "Oh, sorry, Mickey," and shuffled off towards the bathroom. I don't even know if her eyes were open yet.

Mickey smiled.

"Your face feels like mine, I guess," he said. Then he pulled two cups from the cupboard and put them down on the counter and said, "Just pour yourself a cup when it's ready. My dad will be up in a second. He always wakes up early. He's an early riser, I guess. That's what he calls himself, anyway. An early riser."

I said okay and Mickey left.

A few minutes later, Sunny came back. This time she had her glasses on.

"Hello," she said, stepping into the kitchen. I was just standing there, leaning against the counter, watching the water drip into the coffeepot.

"Hi," I said, standing up so my back was straight.

"You left before I got back last night," she said.

She caught me off guard when she said it. I had actually thought of waiting for her, but I wasn't sure how long she was going to be, or if she wanted me to wait for her or not.

It was all pretty confusing.

"Yes, I did," I said. "I wasn't sure if I should wait or not, so –"

"Did you want to wait?" she said, looking at me.

"Yeah, you know. I thought about it."

She smiled.

"Well, I guess that's close enough."

"You want a coffee?" I said, a few seconds later, as if it was mine to offer.

"Sure," she said. I poured her a cup and handed it to her. She took it and sat down in a chair near the tiny kitchen table. She crossed her legs the way adults do all the time and held her coffee with two hands. She still looked pretty tired. Then I poured myself some.

"No walk today?" I said, after taking a few sips.

"We can go for a walk if you want," she said, looking at me.

She surprised me when she said that, too. I had just been referring to the mighty morning walks her and her mom went on all the time, and how it didn't seem like Sunny was going on one this morning.

"Okay. Sure," I said, after thinking for a few seconds.

"Are you sure?" said Sunny. She seemed a bit surprised by my hesitancy, which really wasn't hesitancy at all. I loved the idea of going for another walk with her. I just wasn't used to someone speaking so directly to me. Especially a girl.

"I'm absolutely sure," I said, my excitement starting to show. "When?"

"How about when your classes end?"

"Okay."

"Alright then," she said.

We smiled at each other. Then she took another sip of her coffee, and I took another sip of mine, and I thought to myself that all of a sudden, I had never felt better or more happy in my entire life.

Then Mickey came back from his shower and had something to eat, and he and I went to our writing class together, like a couple of old pals who had known each other for twenty years.

< 4 >

The next three days went by about as well as three days could go by.

I had fun in my writing class. I wrote three stories and a poem. One of my stories was called "The Dog With A Bucket On His Head," which was about this dog I used to know called Gopher that always picked at himself with his teeth until he bled. So, the vet told Gopher's owners (they were friends of Mom and Dad's) that Gopher would have to start wearing this enormous plastic collar that looked like an ice cream pail with the bottom cut out of it.

The start of my story went, *Once upon a time there was a dog named Gopher who wore a bucket on his head. His friends used to tease him all the time, saying things like, "Hey, Bucket-head! Wanna go for an ice cream?" Naturally, Gopher did not like it when they teased him. He would bare his teeth and growl and occasionally try to bite them. But of course, he couldn't get at them, because of the bucket.*

My second story was called "Mayonnaise." It was about a kid who was studying to become a writer. The kid's name was Morris. I don't know where I got that name from. I don't even know where I got the story from. But anyway, here's how it went:

One day, a few of the guys Morris worked with during the summer at the shop asked him about his classes at university. He told them he was studying English.

"English?" said a long, thin rail of a man named Harvey. "You gonna learn all them big, fancy words and try them out on us?"

"No," said Morris, who was in no hurry to talk about his classes with the men he worked with. He figured they wouldn't understand.

"He's gonna learn all them big, fancy words and leave us in the dirt," said Harold, the lower half of whose face was covered with a thick red beard.

"He's gonna be educated," said Gary, smoking another cigarette. "Then he's gonna come back here lookin' to get his job back."

"He's gonna learn all them big, fancy words," said Harvey, again. "Like mayonnaise. Umbrella."

"He's gonna start correcting us all the time," said Harold, scratching his beard.

"No, I'm not," said Morris, who was no more than half the age of the others.

"Sure you are," said Gary, pulling on his smoke.

"Peanut butter," said Harvey.

"That's two words," said Morris.

"See. I told ya," said Gary, starting to laugh.

"You're startin' to correct us already," said Harvey.

"*Peanut butter is two words,*" said Morris, looking exasperated.

"*He's startin' to correct us already,*" said Harvey, again, shaking his head.

My third story was called "Watching Mr. Dressup," which I did every day until I was six years old and had to go to school all day.

On Thursday, we had to write a skit involving two people doing something. It could be about any two people doing any activity, but the whole skit had to be dialogue only. No directions or descriptions or anything.

I wrote about my little pal Henry again. Mr. Happy Shirt. I was babysitting him one day and he wanted to make cookies. I didn't think it was such a terrific idea, but he insisted, and he can be very insistent.

Here's how my story went:

"*Harper, I'm going to put this lego on this cookie sheet, and I'm going to put it into the oven.*"

"*Lego?*"

"*Yes. Lego.*"

"*Good idea.*"

"*Sank you.*"

"*For how long?*"

"*Seventeen minutes.*"

"*Exactly seventeen minutes, or in-the-ballpark seventeen minutes?*"

"*Exactly seventeen minutes.*"

"*Then what?*"

"*I will take them out and blow on them.*"

"*Will you put oven mitts on first?*"

"Yes. First I'll put on oven mitts, and then I'll blow on them."

"And after you blow on them, can I have one?"

"One what?"

"One of those things you're baking in the oven."

"Well, Harper, it's lego. You can't eat them."

"I thought they were cookies."

"I'm just pretending."

"Oh."

"There's real cookies up in the cupboard."

My teacher, Mrs. Dunsforth, told me she liked it.

"It has innocence," she said. "Innocence and humor. That's a rare mix that burns badly when it's overdone. Quite like cookies, actually."

I figured that meant either she was hungry or she'd spent a lot of time in the kitchen.

After everyone had read their story out loud, we had to pair up with someone we had never been with before and evaluate each other's work.

We had done this sort of thing throughout the week and I had always had fun with it. Some of the people took it a bit too seriously. One girl even ran out of the room crying once, after her boyfriend told her her writing was too masculine.

I'm not sure what he meant by that, but she was back in class the next day, so I guess it couldn't have been too bad.

I was matched with this girl, Amber, who, as Henry would put it, had happy hair, meaning she had yellow hair, and an earring through her bottom lip. I could barely look at her without wincing. I don't even like getting needles in my arm, much less one stuck through my lip.

To make it worse, she brought a coffee and a muffin over to our table, so even though I wasn't looking at her, I could hear her opening her mouth and sipping the coffee. All I could think about was her lip ring getting snagged on something and tearing a big hole in her mouth.

She was probably about seventeen, and was one of the people who always sat on the floor instead of on a chair at a table.

Anyway, after she read my story, which we were supposed to do even though we had already listened to all of them, she looked at me and said, "It's very domestic. You know what I mean? Very homey. Very aprons and chocolate chips and flour on your face."

I nodded. I didn't know what to say. I didn't know if she was being critical or paying me the biggest compliment of my life.

Then she went on.

"I think it needs to be taken out of the home. It needs more life. It needs to breathe. The boy should cry out. He should sing. 'I'm making cookies!' What boy wouldn't sing out at a chance like that? What child wouldn't dance and spin and twirl at a chance to make cookies in his mother's kitchen?"

Me, for one, I could have said.

When I was a child, if I ever danced and spun and twirled in my mother's kitchen when the oven was on, I'd be doing twenty minutes to life in my bedroom for being careless and showing disregard for human safety. Not to mention the fact that I'd be skidding out and falling all over the place, since

Mom washed the floor twelve times a day.

Instead I said, "But this really happened. This is a real kid. I'm not making this up."

"Oh, come on, Harper," she said. "Give it some flavor. Open a bottle of your favorite wine and pour it all over your story. Go on. Pop the cork and pour. Then see what you get."

I sat there. I didn't even have any favorite wines. All I drank was Coke.

Then, after a minute or so, she said, "Are you finished?"

"I guess so," I said, with a shrug.

She smiled.

"Good. Now read mine."

She had written about two writers, a man and a woman, both in their early twenties, both students at university who lived together in an apartment overlooking the bistros and bars on Whyte Avenue in Edmonton, who had submitted their manuscripts to the same publisher, and received replies in the mail on the same day.

Here's how her story went:

"Okay. Here they are. Now, you open yours first."

"No. You go first."

"I went first last time."

"I didn't even get a letter back last time."

"Okay. I'll go first. But next time we go out for dinner, you have to order first."

"Alright."

"And you have to remember that."

"Why don't you remember that?"

"Because it's your turn to remember. I remembered that it was my turn to check the mail today."

"Yes. But you forgot to get me a coffee."

"No. It's Wednesday. We don't buy coffee on Wednesday. We buy our coffees on Friday, Saturday, Sunday and Monday. The rest of the time we make our coffee."

"Well, you forgot to make me a coffee."

"No. It's your turn to make the coffee. I made it yesterday."

"Who made breakfast yesterday?"

"You reheated my supper from the night before."

"It was still breakfast."

"It was still my supper."

At this point of my reading, Amber reached over and put her hand on my arm and smiled and said, "Are you sick of them yet?" Her smile was so big I couldn't help but stare at the earring in her lip.

"Not quite," I said. "But I'm getting there."

"Good," she said, patting my arm. "You're right on schedule."

I went back to the story.

"Alright. I'll make the coffee. You open your letter."

"Not until I have my coffee."

"Why don't you open it while I'm making the coffee?"

"Because it's my letter and I can open it when I want."

"Alright. Okay. Fine."

"Thank you."

"And this is my letter and I can open it where I

want, and that's going to be in the bedroom."

"Not before me, it's not."

"Oh yes, before you. I'm going in there right now."

"So am I."

"Well, I'm going first."

"I don't think so."

"Yes, I am."

"No, you're not."

The End.

I put Amber's story down and looked at her. She was beaming, probably because of the sick look I had on my face.

"You're sick of them, right?" she said, with hope in her eyes.

"Yes, I am," I said.

"You want to put them in a space shuttle and send them off to Mars? The first couple in outer space. They'd take care of any other signs of life out there, wouldn't they?"

"So, who are they?" I said. I mean, they had to be somebody.

"You know who they are? That's my mother and her boyfriend, Drake. Can you believe it? That's them today. I turned them into twenty-year-olds to make them a teensy bit more believable. But that's how they talk to each other. Every little issue, every little word, gets blown up into a big deal. And they can take the fun out of anything."

"Did they ever get published?"

"Are you kidding? They're the worst writers on the face of the planet. They make my cats sick. My mom just launched her fourth book last month. Drake's a poet. He's on tour in the States somewhere."

"So they're not the worst writers on the planet?"

"No, unfortunately. I am. I just want them to be."

I told Sunny all about Amber and her story on our walk Thursday night. It had become kind of a regular thing for us, going for walks at night. Sometimes we'd go down to the lake and skip a few rocks and watch the mother ducks herd their ducklings to the shore, or we'd go over to the playground and goof around on the swings. I could never get her to go on the teeter-totters. Neither could Mickey, when he came with us.

One night, the three of us turned the playground into an obstacle course and had races to see who could go through everything the fastest. Mickey and Sunny could just fly across the monkey bars. They said it was because they had a playground near their apartment that had monkey bars in it. They used to have those fights on them all the time, when one person tries to get by the other one.

They had another fight on the monkey bars at camp, I guess for old time's sake. Sunny won when she tickled Mickey's armpit with her foot until he let go.

"Hey, that's cheating," he cried out, when he was still struggling to hang on.

"That's not cheating," said Sunny, who looked like she could hang up there forever.

"She told you to do what?" was her reaction to Amber's suggestion of pouring wine all over my story.

"She said it would add some taste to it. Or flavor. That was the word she used. Flavor," I said.

"I had an art teacher who told me to close my eyes when I painted, so my imagination could run wild. He said young artists always try too hard to be technically sound, and their work always turns out boring," said Sunny.

"What'd you say?"

"I said I would close my eyes when I painted if he closed his eyes when he marked."

She could be pretty funny sometimes.

At around nine o'clock that night we started to head back to her cabin. When it was just barely in sight, Sunny let out a shriek and started running towards it. I didn't know what was going on. I thought maybe she'd seen a bear or something. Or a coyote. So I took off like a madman after her. Then I heard her shouting, "Mom! Mom! You're here! You're here!" and I saw a little blue car parked behind her dad's van in the driveway. I stopped running and hid behind a tree so I could catch my breath and calm my heart down. Then I stepped out and started walking towards the cabin. When I was almost there, the door swung open and Mickey stepped out with this big smile on his face. "Come on in, Harper," he said. "My mom's here. She finally got here. Come on in and say hi."

I stepped inside. Sunny and her mom and dad were clumped together in the tiny kitchen. I walked in and just stood in the doorway for a second. Sunny and her mom were in this big embrace. It was like they hadn't seen each other in a year. Then they separated, and Sunny looked over and saw me and said, "Oh, Harper. I forgot about you. Sorry."

I just kind of smiled and looked at the floor. It's hard to think of something to say when somebody says they've forgotten about you. Besides, it was pretty obvious why she had forgotten, and it's not like she had forgotten my name or anything, or who I was.

Then her mom came towards me.

"So, you're Harper," she said.

She was a couple of inches taller than Sunny and maybe about fifty pounds heavier. She had thick, curly black hair that kind of piled up and fell down the sides of her head, meaning it wasn't combed or gelled or frozen into place with hairspray.

She looked a lot younger than Sunny's dad, but that was probably because he was bald, and going bald never makes a person look younger than he really is, as my dad is slowly starting to discover.

She was wearing sandals and a big, billowy white sundress covered in orange and yellow flowers.

As she walked towards me, she smiled, and I could tell right away that I was going to like her. She had a very fun-looking face. Not funny looking. That's a whole different story. That's Cheryl Tifers, one of my brother William's ex-girlfriends, who had a face like a kangaroo. She had kind of a pointy nose and super-short blond hair and ears that seemed to stick straight up from the top of her head.

I know that's impossible, but that's just the way she looked.

She was from Australia, too, so I imagine that's where the kangaroo thing came from.

"It's very nice to meet you, Harper," said Sunny's mom, holding out her hand. "Sunny has told me a lot about you on the telephone."

She had this big smile on her face. The second I shook her hand I was reminded of a woman I met in my writing class a few years ago. Her name was Del.

"Just the good things, I hope," I said. I hear Mom and Dad saying that all the time, so I guess that's why I said it. I'm usually pretty quiet when it comes to introductions. Anything after "Pleased to meet you" or "Yes, nice to meet you, too" is pretty well a bonus as far as I'm concerned.

"Of course, it's just the good things," said Sunny's mom. "Although she did tell me you ran off without saying goodbye to her one night. And you're not much at Twenty Questions."

I smiled politely and looked at Sunny. She hadn't told her mom any good things, from the sounds of it.

"She did say you wrote a charming little piece about the color yellow that I would love to hear," her mom went on.

"Sure," I said, feeling instantly better. Sunny had never told me she thought my story was charming.

"Good," said her mom. Then she turned to Sunny's dad and said, "Stanley, could you get my bag from the trunk of the car? My back is killing me today. And there's a grocery bag on the side that has to come in. I stopped and did a little shopping on my way out." She turned to me and winked.

Mickey and Sunny looked at each other.

"Potato chips?" said Sunny.

"Jiffy Pop?" said Mickey.

"Campfire food, I prefer to call it," said her mom. "Stanley here doesn't believe in that sort of stuff. So I have to buy it."

"And you, my dear," she added, looking at Sunny, "you forgot your drawing board in the bathroom, of all places."

Sunny made a very dramatic face and clasped her hands around her head

"Ohh," she said in a loud moan. "That's where I left it. I took it in there with me because Dad told me to move it away from the door and I didn't want to forget it. So I took it into the bathroom when I was doing my hair and I left it there. What a nut." Then she looked at her mom and said, with hope in her eyes, "Did you bring it?"

"Right underneath the Cheetohs cheezies," said her mom. "I don't forget a thing when I come on these trips."

Sunny let out a squeal and ran out of the cabin to get it. She went so fast I didn't have a chance to go with her, not that she would be gone for more than about ten seconds.

Then Mrs. Taylor sat down in a chair and looked at Mickey and asked him where his writing was.

"Oh, I've got lots to show you," he said. "I've done a whole bunch of writing this week."

"Well, let me see it."

He zipped off to get it.

You could tell everybody was pretty happy to see her, and that she was happy to be with them. They were all smiling and everything. That's one of the things I noticed about Sunny's family – they all smiled a lot. Even her dad, when his face wasn't buried in a book.

My family doesn't smile nearly that much. Only when my nieces and nephews are around, or if somebody cracks a good joke, which isn't every day. But other than that, there's not much smiling at all. Even when we're all in good moods, no one smiles.

I don't think I had noticed that before.

< 5 >

Friday was the last day of camp. Everyone met at the Rec Hall at eight-thirty for a big special breakfast, the special part being that instead of the teachers sitting at one table and all of us sitting at another, everyone was sitting together and talking and laughing.

I wanted to sit beside Ms. Dunsforth, the woman who told us we'd have to "Think! Think! Think!" all week, but she got swallowed up by Amber, The Girl With The Earring In Her Mouth, and two of her friends before I even had a chance to say hi.

So, instead I ended up sitting with this guy who called himself H. Anthony Gallagher, he always made sure the "H" was in there. He was a writer who was maybe twenty-five years old, wore a black turtleneck everywhere he went, and wrote by candlelight every night at the picnic table outside the bunkhouse I was sleeping in. One night, somebody said to him, "Hey, Mr. H., what's the deal with writing outside in the middle of the night?"

"I am writing about romance," he said. "What

could be more romantic than writing under an open moon by candlelight?"

This got some of the guys going.

"I could tell you," said one of them, who had spent almost the entire week talking about his girlfriend. "How about co-ed bunkhouses?"

"Ever heard of beer?" said another.

"How about co-ed bunkhouses with beer on tap outside the door?" said the first.

Anyway, Anthony told everyone his life story about two days ago during an "open mike" session at lunch. He said that he had always wanted to be a writer and he had tried so hard and had considered quitting so many times. But then, just two months ago, a magazine had accepted one of his stories. Then, a different magazine accepted another one, and three weeks ago, a publisher had written offering him a contract for his manuscript.

Anthony was, in his own words, "aghast with emotion. I was awestruck. I put down the phone and wept in my Gretchen's arms." Gretchen was his girlfriend.

Then he had added, "So you see, my young adult friends, learn from me. Let my story inspire you. Look at me up here now and say to yourselves, 'That is who I want to be. In his footsteps I will travel. In my heart, his story will beat.' Do that, my friends, and you, too, will taste the sweet juices of success, and you will cry the tears of joy, and we can join hands and weep together, brothers in arms, and in our arms will be the pens and quills with which we will tell our stories."

When he finished, I leaned over and said to Mickey, "Like that's what I came here looking for – another brother."

Someone else shouted out, "What's this Gretchen look like?"

Then someone else said, "Yeah, is she part of the deal?"

I guess some of the guys were starting to get a bit lonely as the week wore on.

Then Amber said, "What if you're a woman? What if you don't want to be a brother?"

Anthony never said anything. I'm not even sure if he heard them, he was so caught up in the emotion of the moment.

He seemed a bit closer to the planet earth at breakfast. A big blob of strawberry jam fell on his pants and he nearly gagged on his coffee, it was so hot. He was thoroughly embarrassed and kept apologizing to everyone, even to people who weren't sitting at our table, saying that he had no idea what *spell* he was under, and that if he hadn't packed so quickly this morning, he would have gladly run back to his room to change, so that the others around him would not have to look at the ghastly stain on his pants, or listen to him gurgle and sputter as he drank his "morning wake-up."

I tried to think of the last time I had ever heard anyone use the words "ghastly" and "aghast" in the same week, but I couldn't come up with anyone. Not even my brother's wife, Jennifer, who loves to flex her vocabulary whenever she has the chance. She even says things like, "These are the gloves with which I shovel the drive," or, "There is the man from whom I buy my vegetables and fruit," who is also, incidentally, the same man from whom Mom buys our vegetables and fruit, and he is about the least "from whom" guy you could ever buy anything from in the entire world.

But not even Jennifer has ever used ghastly and aghast back-to-back like that. At least, it seemed like it was back-to-back.

Fortunately, I didn't have to sit beside him for very long. I had just finished dressing up a piece of toast with peanut butter and honey when I was rescued again by Mickey.

"Harper. There you are," he said, walking up to where I was sitting. He was slightly out of breath. Ordinarily, I would have just sat with him, but he had bowed out of breakfast this morning because he wanted to sleep in and then pack. We had all been up pretty late the night before, sitting around the fire and everything. "Sunny wanted me to find you. We're leaving now. We're going. She wants to say goodbye."

"I thought you weren't leaving till noon," I said. Sunny and I had talked about her departure just before I left for the bunkhouse. It wasn't an awful topic or anything. We had already decided that we would see each other again. We had even decided when and where – by the front doors of the library at Churchill Square at noon on Monday.

"My dad wants to get home," said Mickey. "He has to work tonight."

About a minute later I was on the trail with

Mickey back to his cabin, and about an hour after that, I was waving goodbye to Sunny and her mom as they drove away in their little car. Mickey and his dad were just ahead of them.

I felt fine saying goodbye. I hugged Sunny's mom and shook her dad's hand. Then I shook Mickey's hand just because it seemed like the thing to do, even though it felt kind of funny, two kids standing there shaking hands as if we had just closed some major deal.

I didn't know what to do with Sunny, but I didn't have to think about it for very long because she stepped right up and gave me a hug. I hugged her back. I could feel her cheek against my face and her tiny breath on my neck. It felt pretty good, actually.

When we separated, Sunny had a little tear in one of her eyes.

"I've really enjoyed being with you, Harper," she said. "You're a good listener. And I like the way you laugh."

I didn't know what to say to that. Romance is not exactly a well-used language of mine. Not to mention the fact that no one has ever said those things about me before. I should have asked her to wait a minute so I could go find Mr. H. Anthony himself to find out what I should say.

Then she smiled and wiped her nose and said, "Well, I guess I'll see you Monday then," and hopped in the car.

I laughed and said, "Yeah, that's a whole two days away, maybe we should drop each other a letter in between." But I don't know if she heard me.

I stood on the road and waved and watched her and her mom drive around the bend that would take them to the highway. It wasn't long before I couldn't hear their car anymore, and about a minute or so after that, all the dust they had kicked up on the road settled back to where it had been lying, leaving me completely alone for practically the first time all week, or since I first met Mickey outside the Rec Hall.

That was when it really hit me. That was when I knew how much I really liked Sunny, and even everyone else in her family.

I started playing back in my mind all the things she and I had done and all the walks we had gone on. I thought about waking up every morning and going for a shower and then stopping off at their cabin for a coffee and a chat with Sunny or her dad until Mickey was ready to go, and about walking down the path with Mickey and talking about what we thought we'd do in class.

Then I started feeling kind of bad for the way I'd been with Mickey. I mean, he was the first person who said anything to me at this entire camp and he was such a good guy, but all of a sudden I felt like I had snubbed him. You know? Like as soon as I saw Sunny it was as if I said to him, "Excuse me a minute there, Mickey, would you mind stepping back out of my life for a year or two while I go out with your sister?"

I didn't like that feeling at all.

I made a note to myself to phone him when I got home.

Then I thought about playing Twenty Questions. I was actually getting pretty good at it by the time the week was over.

I thought about all that stupid chicken we ate, and all the snacks we had around the campfire last night.

The main thing I thought about, though, was Sunny. I remembered practically every time I made her laugh and how she screamed when I pushed her too high on the swings. "No more under ducks!" she had cried, kicking her feet all over the place.

I knew I was being nostalgic and probably a bit sappy, but I had never felt like this towards anybody before. I really hadn't planned on being that way with her, either. It just happened, I guess.

By the time I made it back to the bunkhouse it was time for everyone to pack and go. Mom said she would pick me up around noon. I took all my stuff and sat on the grass by the parking lot at the Rec Hall. The place was really starting to get busy with cars coming and going and people hanging around waiting.

I recognized just about everyone and I said bye to a few people. I saw the guy with the ponytail and the Walt Whitman book of poetry, but he wasn't singing anymore. He was just sitting by himself on a log, reading his book. I didn't say much to anyone until Amber saw me and waved. I smiled and waved back. She looked about as excited as I was to be going home.

She walked over and was about to say hi when I heard a car horn honk and turned and saw Mom sitting there. She had this look on her face that said she had already been waiting for too long and would I mind getting a move on so she could get back to her own life before everything fell apart.

Apparently, the joy and excitement of sending me to a writing camp had worn off.

Then I saw her look at Amber, from the tip of Amber's yellow hair to the earring in her lip to the curly-toed elf shoes she was wearing. Amber smiled and waved. Then she looked at me and said, "That your mom?"

"Sure is," I said.

"She nice?"

"She can be."

"She sure has a clean car."

"That's how I know it's my mom," I said.

I turned and looked at Mom again. She had a very impatient look on her face now, meaning it was definitely time to get going, so I said goodbye to Amber and carried my bags to the trunk and loaded them in.

Then I opened the passenger door of the car and was about to step in when Amber called out, "Don't forget about the wine!" and made a motion with her hands of pouring wine all over something. I assumed it was the story about cookies made of lego that I had written.

"I won't," I said, and hopped in the car.

Mom gave me a look.

"The wine?" she said. She did not look impressed.

"It's an inside joke," I said. "I'll explain it later."

Mom gave me another look. "I'm sure you will," she said, and put the car in reverse.

< 6 >

Mom told me all about her week on the way home from camp. Gladys Michaels, her executive assistant at the boutique, which is a fancy way of saying the person who watches the till when Mom goes to the bathroom or gets tied up on the phone with a customer, put in her two-week notice again. This will be the fourth time in the last year that Gladys has decided to quit. Mom keeps praying for the day when it actually happens, but so far it hasn't, and she doesn't think this time will be any different.

Mom doesn't like Gladys. Gladys eats chunks of garlic sausage the size of chocolate bars at least twice a week for lunch, and she doesn't exactly pull out the Colgate to brush her teeth when she's done, so her breath is pretty strong, to say the least. And her husband, Alvin, always drops by for coffee and stays for half a day. Alvin is a truck driver. He's on the road all the time, down to California or Texas or back east to Ontario or the Maritimes, so quite often, the only time he even sees Gladys is when she's in the store.

Mom said that the two of them sit in the fancy chairs outside the change rooms and talk and giggle and carry on like *teenagers*, making teenagers sound like some kind of beetle that nests in the pockets of new clothing, or eats through the wood on all the hangers.

Then she told me that the Newsomes, Mom and Dad's best friends, were moving to Phoenix, and had invited Mom and Dad to join them, but of course, Mom and Dad couldn't because, as Mom put it, "we still have a family to raise," meaning me.

This was a bit much to take.

"So, Dad would quit being a doctor and you would hand your store over to Gladys and move down to Phoenix if I wasn't around?" I said.

"I would not hand the store over to Gladys," said Mom, taking her eyes off the road to look at me, which emphasized the importance of what she was saying. "I would get rid of that woman in a second if I could. Unfortunately for me, eating garlic sausage is not yet considered suitable grounds for dismissal. She doesn't even use a napkin. Lord knows what she wipes her hands on when she's finished with it."

"But you would actually go there if it wasn't for me?" I said, again. She had obviously missed the point the first time around.

This time Mom sighed and shook her head.

"No, we probably wouldn't, and it's not because of you. This has just been a very awful week."

Then she told me the capper. My brother,

William, and his wife, Jennifer, were "having a few problems getting along."

"Meaning what?" I said. Everybody has problems getting along with William. That's why I sent him a thank-you card a little while ago for moving out of the house as early as he did.

I didn't really, but I could have. I certainly felt like it.

"They've decided to separate. William has moved into a motel in the west end of the city. Jennifer is staying in the home."

"What about the kids?" I said. William could be staying in a motel room in the west end of Mars for all I cared. And I really wasn't all that fussy about Jennifer, either. But the kids … they were terrific.

"They're staying with Jennifer. William misses them terribly."

"How long as he been out for?"

"Three days. He left last week. They've been talking about it for months. I don't know what made them finally decide to do it."

"I'll bet he didn't see them for much more than an hour every three days when he was at home, anyway," I said, which was probably not what Mom wanted to hear.

William is like Dad when it comes to work, which means that to both of them, Work is Life, and Life is Work, and everything else comes second.

She looked at me again.

"That's what the problems are about," she said. She looked very sad all of a sudden. "You never know with these things. If they'll work it out or not.

So many couples today are getting divorced."

It was at that exact moment that I decided to tell her about Sunny. I don't know why I felt that way, except I was already tired of talking about my brother.

"I met a girl at this camp you sent me to," I said.

I was staring straight ahead when I said it, because I didn't have the nerve to look at Mom's reaction. But after I said it, I had to look at her.

She didn't say anything. She didn't look at me. She just kept driving down the highway and checking all her mirrors like she always does, making sure that no one was flying up behind her. She really doesn't like highway driving very much.

Then, after about a minute, she said, "I'm sorry. What was that, dear?"

I guess she had been lost in thought.

"I said, I met a girl at this camp you sent me to." This time she did look at me.

"What do you mean you met a girl? You mean, there was a girl up there you enjoyed writing with? There was someone up there who writes the way you do?"

"No. I mean I met a girl. A girl girl. She doesn't write at all. She's an artist. She was there with her brother and her dad."

Mom went silent. You could tell she was thinking.

"A girl girl," she said.

She tightened her grip on the steering wheel. Then, all of a sudden, she looked at me with an expression of sheer dread on her face and said, "Not that girl you said goodbye to at the parking lot, with the yellow hair and those ridiculous shoes and the earring through her mouth."

She was talking about Amber.

"No, no. Not her," I said, thinking that it would have been awfully interesting if it was.

"Well, I'm relieved to hear that," said Mom, looking relieved.

"So, tell me about her. What's her name?" she said, a few seconds later. You could tell she was trying to stay cool and make sense of everything that was going on, and with one son moving away from his family, and another son coming home from a week in the woods with news that he's met a girl, there was a fair bit to deal with.

"Sunny," I said.

She closed her eyes and opened them and took another deep breath. I knew she wasn't going to like Sunny's name. It's one of those "nature" names that always drives Mom nuts, like Forrest and Rain and Autumn.

"And she was there with her father?"

"Yes," I said. I knew what was coming next.

"What does he do?"

That was it. Mom always asks what people do for a living. It's as if she can't make the decision whether she likes them or not until she knows. It really drives me crazy.

"He's a stripper," I said. I had been planning that answer for days. "A male stripper. One of the best, too, from what I hear."

Mom looked at me. I could tell it was not the time to joke. I also knew that my news of having a girlfriend was pretty small compared to William moving out. From her point of view, anyway.

She was pretty quiet for a while after that, so quiet that I was tempted to say, "No, he's not a stripper. He's a librarian," but I didn't because under the circumstances, I wasn't sure if she would believe me about his real occupation, either. I mean, how many librarians do Mom and Dad associate with? None. And male librarians? Even less.

"You're not going to tell me?" she said, finally.

She may have been upset with my answer, but she wasn't going to let go of the question.

"He's a librarian," I said. I had to give in sometime. "He works downtown at the reference desk. He's been there forever. Her mom works at home. She's a freelance writer, or something. And a teacher. Sunny and her brother go to school at home. They're home schoolers."

Mom's eyebrows went so far up when she heard all of that, they practically fell off the top of her head.

I couldn't tell for sure what she was thinking, but I figured it was something along the lines that I had become hooked up with one of these new-age families who gave their kids silly names and questioned everything that had ever been done before and believed in herbal medicine instead of going to the doctor's, which, in my dad's case, was bad for business.

"Is she sick?" said Mom, with a concerned look on her face all of a sudden.

"Sick?" I said. Where did that come from?

"Yes. This girl you're seeing. Is she sick? Does she have an illness of some kind, like asthma? Or is she shy? I know of some people who home school because their kids just don't get along with others very well. They're a little bit shy or too sensitive. Mavis Jenson's daughter used to cry all the time when they left her alone in Sunday School. I think they considered home schooling at some point. Of course, it wasn't as popular then as it is now. You know how these fads work."

I rolled my eyes and looked out the window. I felt like saying to her, "Yes, Mom, this girl I'm seeing, whose name happens to be Sunny, by the way, is sick and shy and she cries all the time, but that's what makes her so special."

But instead I said, very calmly, "No, Mom. She is not sick or shy, and the only time I saw her cry was when she told me about her aunt who's dying from cancer because her doctor messed up and made a mistake."

Mom looked at me again. This time she really meant business. Criticizing the medical profession was an absolute no-no around our house. It was even worse than walking across the kitchen floor with your shoes on, or putting your feet up on the couch.

She bore about six dozen holes into me with her eyes, then she said, "I hope you didn't just stand there and say nothing after you heard that."

It was our family honor she was talking about now. She wanted to hear how I unsheathed my sword and cried for the head of the speaker of such words, and if fifty masked bodyguards appeared before me, how I took them all on, with the badge of my father's business card, complete with home and office phone numbers, emblazoned on my chest.

"I think the chicken got there before I could say anything," I said, after thinking about it for a second.

"The chicken?" said Mom. This was not the way she usually liked to get her information, in random little bits that seemed to go on forever.

"Sunny ordered Kentucky Fried Chicken for the week. Fifty bucks' worth. They delivered it right to the campsite."

Mom shook her head and went back to her driving.

We drove on in complete silence for about half an hour after that. Then I remembered something that I wanted to say to her. Sunny and I had talked about it on one of our walks.

"Thanks for sending me," I said.

I was pretty sure I had thanked her and Dad before, but I thought I should do it again, especially since I had enjoyed myself so much, and because I had met Sunny there.

Mom looked at me again. She just stared at me for a second, then a little smile crept across her face.

"You're welcome," she said, shaking her head again. "Sounds like you had a very interesting time."

"I did," I said, nodding and smiling.

I felt really good all of a sudden, and I think Mom did, too, for some reason.

"You're going to see her again when you get home, I imagine?" she said.

"Monday at noon," I said.

Mom's eyebrows went up again.

"My, my. You've made plans already. This sounds like someone your father and I should meet."

The smile I had on my face froze. I looked over at Mom. Was this some kind of trap she had set for me, or what?

"Are you ready for that one yet?" she said. Her eyes were beaming and she had a full-fledged smile on her face, and it was gaining momentum. "Dinner at Mom and Dad's? I could tuck her right in beside me and tell her everything about you. We could do the dishes together. Go for a walk. I could teach her to sew, if she doesn't know already."

She looked as excited as I've ever seen her, and worst of all, she seemed to be genuine about it.

I, on the other hand, felt sick. Introducing Sunny to Mom and Dad? Now? Before I even had a chance to sit down and tell her all about them?

To top it off, there was no way I could answer her. I couldn't even open my mouth, much less say anything, which I guess was exactly the response she was looking for.

"That'll teach you for eating fifty dollars' worth of chicken, now won't it?" she said.

She went on smiling and driving all the way home.

< 7 >

Sunny was waiting for me when I got to the library on Monday. She was wearing her blue jean overalls and a t-shirt and sandals. She had this big straw sun-hat on her head and a great big bag over her shoulder. She waved like crazy when she saw me get off the bus.

The first thing she said to me was, "Guess what?"

"What?" I said.

It was kind of funny that I said that, actually. For the past day and a half, I'd spent practically all my time thinking about the first thing I would say to her when I saw her again, or the first thing I would do when I saw her, and all of a sudden, there I was, stepping off the bus with her coming towards me, and the first word out of my mouth was, "What?"

Not very creative, I can tell you.

"I made us lunch," she said, patting the bag. "We can eat it over there at the park." She pointed across the street. "Isn't this terrific weather? I could have worn shorts, it's so nice out."

We walked across the street to the park. Actually, it's called a Square. It's this big grassy area right downtown with benches and walkways. Sometimes there are bands playing music, or food vendors selling french fries and hamburgers and just about anything else you can cook in a van or a bus that's been turned into a kitchen. It can get pretty crowded on days when the sun is out, especially when there's a festival on.

We walked until Sunny stopped in her tracks and said, "This is the spot. Right here is perfect." Then she laid this little blanket on the ground and we sat down and she started pulling food out of her bag. She had two pumpernickel bagels wrapped in baggies and a bunch of things to put on them, like cream cheese, tomato and cucumber slices, and this tiny little tupperware container of chicken salad. Then she pulled out some carrots and celery sticks and cookies, for dessert.

"So, what do you think?" she said, when everything was laid out on the blanket.

"It looks like the start of National Health Week here," I said. I couldn't believe it. Where was Mom when I wanted her? Or, at least, where was a camera so I could take a picture?

"My mom figured you might need a break after a week full of chicken," said Sunny. "I got everything ready this morning."

"Thank you," I said. I had thought we were just going to buy something.

"You know what else I have?" she said, reaching into her bag. She had this huge smile on her face.

"Some vinegar for the bagels?" I said, as a joke, thinking back to that guess she had made with the Kentucky Fried Chicken delivery guy.

"This," she said, and she handed me this little drawing, maybe about a 5" x 7", of a tiny little yellow t-shirt with a happy face on it. Beneath it were the words, in the awkward print of a five-year-old, "Love, Henry."

I couldn't take my eyes off it when she showed it to me. I thought it was beautiful, and by far the most meaningful gift I'd ever gotten in my life.

"I printed with my left hand so I would get it right," she said. "Just guessed at the t-shirt. Does that look like the one he was wearing?"

"It's perfect," I said. I still couldn't believe she had done this for me.

"I'll do another one, if you want," she said, nonchalantly, as if she had just handed me a pair of socks.

"Don't you just love bagels?" she went on, reaching for a bagel. I guess she wanted to move on from the gift. "There used to be this little place on Whyte Avenue that sold nothing but bagels. They had the wildest fillings for sandwiches there. Or toppings. You could put anything you wanted on your bagel."

I thought about that for a second.

"Spaghetti?" I said. I was in such a good mood. Especially now. Yesterday had felt like the longest day in the history of the world.

"No. Not spaghetti."

"Corn flakes and milk?"

"No. Not corn flakes and milk. But they did have

breakfast bagels that came with any kind of egg you wanted, plus bacon or ham, or peanut butter and jam, or even honey, if you wanted that."

"My dad likes peanut butter and bacon sandwiches," I said, picking up the cucumbers.

"Mine likes anything with mustard. Anything at all you could put on a sandwich, with a little squirt of mustard on top of it. He even had a peanut butter and jam sandwich with mustard once, on a dare. My mom dared him to do it. And he had to eat the whole thing, which he did, but he didn't like it. That's the one sandwich he won't eat with mustard."

I stared at Sunny while she was talking. She was building herself a sandwich and going on and on about her dad and his mustard.

I couldn't believe how easily we just fell in step with each other, or how terrific she looked in her sunhat, with her bare little white arms, or how glad I was to be with her again.

She seemed so comfortable in the city, too. She just marched across the street to this little patch of the park we were sitting on and laid out the blanket and sat down, while I looked all over the place for buses and cars and stared at all the interesting people I saw. And for some of them, "interesting" was putting it mildly.

We talked about a million things while we ate our lunch. She told me about her day yesterday with her Auntie Mavis, the one who has cancer, and how, at the end of their visit, her aunt had said that she wanted to meet me.

"That's quite the honor, you know," said Sunny.

"This woman is dying. She only spends time with people she wants to be with. For her to say she wants to meet you … that's something. That's pretty good. Of course, I did put in a good word for you. I also told her how you ditched me one night after my shower and pushed me too high on the swings, but all she said was, 'That's okay. Boys are like that, sometimes.'"

I nodded.

"She's right. We are like that sometimes." Then I added, "Did you happen to tell her how you cheated at Twenty Questions?"

Sunny gave me a look.

"I didn't cheat."

"And how you slurped all the gravy we ordered in one gulp and ate the skin off all the chicken before anybody else could have a piece?"

"That's disgusting. I didn't do that."

"I'm going to tell her you did."

"You are not. I didn't do any of that. I took the skin off my chicken. I get sick eating that."

"Well, I didn't do that other stuff."

"She thinks you did."

"Well, I'll just have to take her to a playground and show her what a gentleman I am."

"She'd like that, I bet. If she could go."

We talked about the movies and books and where we buy our clothes. I told her Mom buys most of the things I wear.

"She knows all about that kind of stuff," I said, truthfully, even though I don't wear half the things she brings home. "That's her 'Area of Expertise,' as she calls it. She put my dad through med school making clothes for people."

"Sounds like you have a cool mom," said Sunny, picking up the carrots.

I stopped chewing a bite of my sandwich and looked at her.

"What?" I said.

"Sounds like you have a cool mom. I'd love to know more about clothes. Look at me. This is my entire wardrobe – overalls and t-shirts. Plus, for the summer, I have two pairs of shorts, and a sundress. In the winter I put on a long jacket to cover everything up. My mom doesn't even know which end of the needle you put the thread through. My dad has never been in a changeroom in his life. He walks into a store, sees something on the rack, buys it, brings it home, and wears it. Then he goes shopping again the next year. Mickey would walk around all day in his underwear if Mom didn't go shopping for him. She even has to buy him that."

"No one has ever called my mom cool before," I said, as if I was stating a fact, which I was.

"Well, I think she sounds pretty cool."

"Not even my dad," I said.

Then Sunny changed the subject.

"Hey, you want to read a good book? I should have thought of this one last week at camp when we were playing our game. You guys would still be guessing. It's called *The Animal Family* by Randall Jarrell."

"*The Animal Family*?" I said.

"Yes. I even bought it new, and I don't do that

very often. I'm more of a used-book person."

"A true story?"

"No. Not quite. But it's very good, and it has lots of these cute little drawings in it. It's about a hunter and a mermaid and all of these animals they meet."

"A hunter and a mermaid?"

"You have to use your imagination."

I thought about that for a second, then I said, "You like books about animals, don't you?" I was referring to how she and Mickey had read *Watership Down* as part of their schooling.

"Sometimes."

"What's your favorite? *Black Beauty*?"

"I would have to say *The Animal Family* is, at the moment."

"What about *Moby Dick*?"

"It's a very good book. Very imaginative."

"Or Bugs Bunny? Have you ever read *The Complete Works Of Bugs Bunny*?"

"I haven't read *Moby Dick*. It's too old and too long. I don't know how anybody could write a book so long about a whale. *Black Beauty* was okay."

"What about Bugs Bunny?"

Sunny looked at me. We were both having so much fun just being there together. I was even starting to get silly I was so happy. Or maybe I was silly from the moment I stepped off the bus and saw her standing there at the library.

"What about Bugs Bunny?"

"Haven't you ever studied Bugs Bunny?"

Sunny rolled her eyes.

"No. I guess I'm not ready for him yet. Or her. What is Bugs Bunny, anyway, a boy or a girl?"

"What about The Coyote? What a life he's had. Tragedy. Failure. But he keeps plugging away, trying to achieve his ultimate goal. Trying to catch that crazy Roadrunner."

"Uh-huh," said Sunny, nodding her head. "And how about you, Mr. Hilarious? What kind of books do you read?"

"Anything over two hundred pages," I said, switching to my serious voice. "I have no time for skinny novels. If it's not an epic journey or a struggle of some kind, or a classic, I don't want it. I won't even light my pipe for it. I'll just sit there in my rocking chair and rock. I won't even pick it up."

"Light your pipe," said Sunny. She was smiling. I know she was having fun, too. "I'd like to see you in a rocking chair with a pipe in your mouth. You'd be coughing so much. I don't even know why people smoke pipes."

"My grandpa used to. He'd sit there and spend an hour lighting the thing, then lean back in his chair and just puff away. Very contented."

"And that's how you want to be? Puffing away in a rocking chair all day?"

"In front of a window, so I could see all the kids going to school. And with Herbie on my lap, for company. Herbie is my dog, by the way."

"Does he smoke a pipe, too?"

"No," I said. "He chews tobacco. It's quite disgusting. I don't know how Mom puts up with him."

"I suppose you'd have a stack of five-hundred-page books beside you?" said Sunny, moving away from Herbie before I could tell her how he spits into his own spittoon.

"Absolutely," I said.

"And your mom out buying you clothes?"

"And you out ordering me chicken. With a side order of skin, for yourself, of course. And a tub of gravy, for dipping."

She threw at carrot at me for that last bit.

After we finished eating, we packed up our lunch and went and said hi to her dad in the library. He was on the phone when we got there, but he gave us a big wave and asked for us to wait for him.

I liked Mr. Taylor. He gave Sunny a hug when he got off the phone and asked us how our lunch was, meaning she had probably told him about it and he had actually remembered.

"It was wonderful," said Sunny.

"Except she ate almost everything," I said.

We all laughed. That's when I knew I felt comfortable around her dad, when I told a joke in front of him. Usually I don't say anything that even has a chance of being funny until I know somebody for about a year. And you can double that where an adult is involved.

The other thing I liked about him was, he absolutely loved books. They were his whole life, aside from his family. Practically every time I saw him at the writing camp, he had a book in his hand. I think he had about three different ones on the go while he was there. Sunny told me he does that because sometimes he's not in the mood for a particular kind of book, but he still feels like reading, so he'll start another book, and go with it until he feels like going back to the first one again, or starting up another one.

We visited with him for a few more minutes. He told us he was working late and wouldn't be around for supper. Then Sunny and I walked down Jasper Avenue until we got to the theaters. Sunny asked me if I felt like seeing a movie. It was right around two o'clock, so the matinees were just starting.

You would not believe how excited I got when she asked me that.

My friend Billy and I always go to the movies together, but he was away at a camp for almost the entire summer, so I figured I was either going to miss them, or have to get used to going alone.

But the sudden burst of happiness and excitement I felt went beyond having a buddy to see movies with. I was just really enjoying my time with Sunny. We had so many things in common and we could talk so easily with each other.

I leaned over and put my arm around her shoulder and gave her a big hug right there on the sidewalk. I caught her completely off guard. She didn't even have time to move her arms or anything. But I had to do it.

It was the first time in my life that I had ever initiated a hug with someone who was not a relative, and even then when I did it, it was only because of what Mom would say later if I didn't.

Then I did something that surprised Sunny almost as much as it surprised me, or so I thought, initially. I kissed her.

I was still holding her in this sort-of-a-hug position and her face was right there in front of mine with this expression that said, "Would you mind telling me what you're doing?" when I moved about an inch closer and planted a kiss right on her lips. Then I pulled back and looked at her, and did it again.

Then I stood back and released her from my hug.

We stared at each other for a few seconds, then she kind of smoothed her clothes a bit and cleared her throat and smiled.

"I was wondering when we were going to do that," she said. Those were the first words she said after I kissed her.

"You were?" I said. I was surprised. I was expecting something like, "My, aren't you the smooth operator."

"Sure. I thought we were going to make out at camp."

"Really?" I said.

I hadn't even really thought of it at camp, probably because every time I saw her, she was with either her dad or Mickey.

"I was ready to," she said.

I stared at her for a second. Then I said, "So was I."

"I wonder why we didn't then," said Sunny. Then she looked over at the theater we had been planning to go into and said, "Come on. Let's go see what's playing."

I hesitated.

"I don't want to see a movie now," I said. I still had the taste of her lips on my mouth. They tasted wonderful.

"We don't have to watch it," said Sunny, and she looked at me with this funny little smile on her face, and then, all of a sudden, I got the picture, and we went inside to the movie.

< 8 >

The movie we went to was called *Jerry McGuire*, starring Tom Cruise. It wasn't new or anything. I guess the theater people just decided to run it again because so many people liked it the first time around.

Sunny and I went straight up to the balcony and sat in practically the last row. We didn't stop in the lobby. We didn't buy any popcorn or pop. It was the first movie I had ever been to in my life where I didn't buy popcorn and pop. Not even small ones that you can eat and drink before you even get to your seat.

When we sat down we just looked at each other and started making out. I couldn't believe it. I had never done anything like this before and all of a sudden it was like my life would be over if we stopped.

We were kissing like crazy and I kept running my hands along her bare arms and around her back. She felt so small and fresh and gorgeous. I felt tingles and shivers all over my body. I didn't even notice those stupid armrests they have in those chairs in the theaters. I couldn't tell you the name of even one of the previews they showed.

I was just starting to think about maybe trying something else when all of a sudden, Sunny pulled away from me and said, "Oh-oh, I think I lost a contact lens."

I moved back.

"What?" I said. I was still caught up in the magical marathon kiss we had going, not to mention the excitement of feeling her body in my arms.

"I think I lost a contact lens," she said again, this time with urgency. She was blinking like crazy, and she was trying to look at her fingers on her right hand, I guess to see if anything was stuck to them.

"You think you lost a what?" I said again. I was still on my way down from another world.

"A contact lens. It was bugging me, so I went to fix it and it came right out on my finger. Now I can't find it."

I looked at her, then I looked at the giant movie screen in front of us, but I wasn't really looking at it, then I looked back at her.

"You went to fix your contact lens and it came off on your finger?" I said.

"Yes."

"When?"

"When?"

"Yes. When. When did you do all this?"

"When do you think? About two minutes ago." She was starting to get mad.

"What are you doing fixing your contact lens when you're making out?" I said. I was starting to get a little mad myself. I mean, you could have poked out both my eyes with a stick and I wouldn't have noticed, but she felt a little itch somewhere and went looking for it with her finger, and now this.

"Can you see if it's on my face?" she said, ignoring my question, and sticking her face in my face. "On my cheek? Sometimes it just slips off my finger and sticks to whatever it lands on."

I gave a token look at her cheek.

"I don't see anything," I said.

"What about my hand. My fingers. Can you look? I'm blind without these things."

I looked at her hand and her fingers.

"Up close," she said, and she practically shoved her hand in my face.

I can tell you with all honesty that I really did not feel like looking for the stupid thing. Or finding it. Not the way I was feeling at the moment.

"Is it there?" she said.

"Not that I can see."

"Are you looking?"

"Of course, I'm looking. What else would I be doing? Making out?"

"Check on my pants."

I looked at her pants. I couldn't see anything, but the way I was looking, there could have been a forty-pound dog sitting there wagging its tail and sticking its big wet nose in my face and I would have said, "No, I don't see anything."

"Look hard, please. I have to find it."

I sat back in my chair and stopped looking.

"Sunny, can I ask you something?"

She was still looking all over the place, although with only one good eye and all the lights out around her, I couldn't imagine her finding something that has no color and is about the size of a miniature dime.

"Can you help me look for my contact lens?" she said.

"I will. In a second."

"I'm dead if I don't find it," she went on. "Come on. Help me look for it. Maybe it's on your shirt. Or on your arm."

I looked at her again.

"Sunny. We're in a movie theater. How are we going to find a contact lens in a movie theater, especially with all the lights off?"

She looked at me. One eye was now completely shut, but still twitching. The other one was blinking and trying to focus.

"Harper. That's the only set of contact lenses I have, okay? My parents aren't buying me new ones. They don't like them in the first place because they're too expensive, and in the second place, my mom thinks they're too easy to lose. So we either find it, or I walk around like this for the rest of the day until I put on my glasses, and I hate my glasses."

"Would that mean no more kissing?" I said, sort of as a joke, but not completely.

Sunny just looked at me. She didn't say a word. She just looked at me.

I started to look for her contact lens. I looked down at the floor. It was pitch black. I looked at my seat and along my arms.

"You have to feel, with your fingers," she said.

I started to feel along my arm with my fingers. I couldn't feel anything, except all the goosebumps going away that had been covering my body about five minutes ago.

"Is it in your eye?" I said. I've heard of that happening before. A person thinks they've lost their contact, when really, it's still in their eye, just in a different place.

"No, it's not in my eye," she said.

So much for that.

We looked in silence for about another minute, then she said, "Well, forget this. Let's get out of here. Maybe it's on my clothes somewhere."

I turned and looked at her again and was about to say something like, Well, let's stay for a bit longer. Maybe it's here somewhere, because I was really dying to kiss her again, but she was already standing up. She had her bag in her hand and everything. She even put her hat on.

Outside the theater, in the sunshine of the afternoon, I found her contact lens sitting right there at the bottom of her cheek, right beside her mouth. One more kiss and I probably would have eaten it, or, at least, taken it into my mouth and thought, What on earth is this?

Sunny was incredibly relieved. She had some contact lens solution in her bag, so she just popped into a bathroom at one of the restaurants along Jasper Avenue and put it back into her eye.

When she came out she had this big, super-looking smile on her face.

"Whew," she said. "I'm glad that's over. Come

on. Let's go to my place."

I was glad she had her lens back in her eye, but with all the excitement over, if you could call it that, and I'd rather not, since to me the excitement ended when she lost the thing, I still wanted to ask her something.

"So, Sunny," I said, as we walked along the sidewalk. "What were you doing rubbing your eye when we were making out?"

She looked at me.

"What do you mean, 'What was I doing?' I was rubbing my eye. It was itchy."

"I mean, what were you doing even thinking about your eye? You could have poked both my eyes out with a stick and I wouldn't have felt anything." I liked that line from when I thought of it before.

"I'll try that next time," she said, with a smile.

"I mean it. What were you doing thinking about your eye? Did it just get super-itchy all of a sudden, or were you just kind of phasing out of our kiss for a minute and realized your eye hurt?"

She looked at me. I think she knew what I was getting at.

"Harper, your kisses were delightful, alright. I loved them, and I want to do it with you again and again and again. But those weren't exactly the most comfortable chairs in the world in there. And the movie was very loud. And yes, my eye became super-itchy all of a sudden, as you put it, although it had been bugging me for most of the day. Plus, I was getting thirsty."

"Thirsty?" I said.

"Yes. I was getting thirsty."

"Who gets thirsty making out?"

"I do. It dries out my mouth, I guess. I don't know. What's wrong with getting thirsty?"

"There's nothing wrong with it. I just don't see how you could be aware of it," I said. I hadn't been aware of anything. Tom Cruise could have stepped out of the movie and walked over and watched us for five minutes and I wouldn't have even noticed he was there. They could have turned all the lights on and I wouldn't have noticed it.

"Well," said Sunny, "it's not like making out on a couch, alright? On a couch, I'm not thinking about anything else. But in a movie theater, with the smell of popcorn all around me, and those lousy chairs, and an itchy eye … I thought I did pretty good. We both did."

I stopped walking.

Sunny walked on for about ten steps before she realized she was walking alone. Then she stopped, turned around, looked at me, and said, "Now what are you doing?"

I walked towards her.

"On a couch?" I said, as if I was an investigator who had just heard the slip-up of the century.

"I said that, yes," said Sunny, nodding.

"You've made out with someone on a couch before?"

I started to get a picture in my mind, but I had to block it out.

"Haven't you?" she said.

I stopped walking again. My mind was swirling

– 104 –

around in fifty different directions. But now I had a problem.

I gulped and licked my lips.

"Yes," I said, trying to sound casual.

"Well? If you can, why can't I?" said Sunny.

Of course she had a point. It would be different if she knew that I was lying. At least, I think it would be different. Maybe it wouldn't be.

"With who?" I said.

"With who, what?" said Sunny.

"With who did you kiss on the couch?"

Sunny shook her head.

"Harper, I'm almost seventeen years old, okay? I've kissed a few boys in my day. But the one guy I've actually made out with before was named Stanley. He used to live on the same floor as me. In our apartment."

"What happened to him?" I said, quite clearly, even though my head was spinning. *Kissed a few boys in my day*? Who was this woman?

"Oh, we broke up about two years ago. He was a drip. Then he moved, so I hardly even see him anymore."

"Where'd he move to?" I said, feeling better. But not completely better.

"The main floor. His mom has a bad leg or hip or something."

I stopped walking again. For some reason, I couldn't ask questions and walk at the same time.

"He's still in your building?" I said, as if she had just told me that there was some criminal living there.

"Yes," she said, turning to give me a funny look. "Is there a problem with that?"

Yes, I felt like saying.

"No," I said, and started walking again.

What a date this was turning out to be.

"So, who have you kissed?" said Sunny, after a minute or so. "Anyone I know?"

"Nope," I said, thankful for the out she had given me. I had no idea who I would have come up with as my make-believe kisser. Maybe Amber from my writing class, except she had an earring in her mouth, so I don't even know if she would be eligible or not. Or Veronica, this girl from high school whose boyfriend wanted to twist my head with a socket wrench last year. But the last time I saw Veronica, she was wearing blue lipstick, and I really could not imagine kissing anyone wearing blue lipstick.

"Does she live in your building?" said Sunny.

She was kidding me now. She knows I live in a house.

I appreciated her making light of everything. I guess it really wasn't a big deal.

"Not anymore," I said. "She moved out a week ago."

"Bad breakup?" said Sunny.

I looked at her. She was kind of laughing and so was I. I think right at that moment I felt love for the very first time in my life. True, outside-of-the-family love.

"She went back to her husband in Paris," I said.

Sunny looked at me with this very serious look on her face.

"Did he pay you off? Did he give you a million dollars in exchange for his wife, whom he discovered he loved after all?"

"No. She just ran out of clean laundry and had to go home," I said.

We put our arms around each other and laughed and walked in a zigzag along the sidewalk to her apartment.

I couldn't wait to lie down with her on her couch.

< 9 >

We ended up having supper with Mrs. Taylor.

Mickey had taken the bus to their Auntie Mavis's house and Mr. Taylor, as he had told us, was working late. But Sunny's mom was home and was very happy to see us, as we were to see her, more or less.

She invited me over for supper and I said yes and phoned home and left a message.

Sunny and I made a big tossed salad and a pot of tortellini with pasta sauce they had frozen in their freezer. Sunny told me it was her favorite meal – tortellini and salad.

The three of us sat and ate in the kitchen and talked about our day and the beautiful weather and the submission her mom was preparing to send to a magazine.

When we finished, her mom asked if we felt like going for another walk, so out we went again, this time to a little coffee bar down the street that had tables and chairs on the sidewalk.

It must have been a regular spot because her mom

knew just about everyone who walked by, and Sunny knew about half of them.

"Hello there, Joe," her mom said to this old guy sitting at a table when we walked outside with our coffee. "How's Elsie today? How's she feeling?"

Old Joe nodded for about three minutes before he said anything. He had just taken a sip of coffee when Sunny's mom asked him her question, and he was taking a long time to swallow it. Still, I thought it was pretty neat, this guy in his seventies, or maybe even his eighties, sitting at an outdoor bistro, as Sunny called it, sipping a coffee that had all of this whipped cream and chocolate shavings all over the top of it.

"Not so bad. Not so bad," he said, slowly, nodding his head.

"Good, good," said Sunny's mom. "Tell her I said hi."

"I will," said Joe. "I'll be seeing her again in the morning." He looked at me and nodded a hello. "They tell me she'll still be there in the morning."

"Poor guy," said Sunny's mom, after we sat down. "He's so lonely. Married sixty-two years to the same beautiful woman and when they need each other the most, she's in a room in the hospital and he's alone in their apartment."

Then she said hi to a man who rode up on his mountain bike. He was wearing spandex shorts and a cycling shirt, shoes, gloves, and a helmet.

"Stephan," she said, her mood much brighter. "When are you going to be like the rest of us and trade in that bicycle of yours for a pair of slippers and some reading glasses?"

Stephan got off his bike. He was very tanned and had long, blond hair. From a distance, he looked like he was probably about twenty-five, but up close, you could see by the lines in his face that he was at least twice that.

He walked over to where we were sitting and said, "You know what the young ladies call me when they see me on my bike? They say, 'Oh, oh, here comes Goldilocks. Hello, Goldilocks.' I tell them that I'm Goldilocks and Papa Bear all rolled into one."

We laughed.

"Oh yeah? Well, when are you gonna sit still and start eating some porridge?" said Sunny's mom. "You're gonna get hurt on that crazy thing."

Stephan laughed and shook his head.

"Did I ever tell you that on the day I was born, my mother rode her bike two miles to our neighbor's house, the Erikssons, I believe they were called, I can't remember now, because the midwives were already there, catching a new baby for Mrs. Eriksson. That's how the midwives described their role. I'll never forget that. They used to say, 'We don't deliver babies. We catch them.' Anyway, my mother left my brothers and sisters at home under the care of Anders, my oldest brother, who must have been about fourteen at the time, and rode with me kicking and twirling in her belly to the neighbors, rang the bell on her bicycle, stepped off, and went inside the door."

"Wow," said Sunny. She had this very amazed look on her face.

"I don't doubt that, Stephan," said her mom. "You old Europeans would do anything to make a story interesting. But tell me this. Were you conceived on a bicycle?"

"Mom!" said Sunny, suddenly embarrassed, but laughing at the same time.

"Because if you were," her mom went on, "I will leave you alone and never hassle you again about riding your bike. I may even get one for myself. Two of them. I suppose Larry should come along. Of course, we'd have to have a little book bag with us."

"I wasn't conceived on a bicycle," said Stephan, shaking his head. "But when my daughters started after me about meeting new people after my wife Rosie died, I went to dances and joined clubs and started volunteering here and there. Never met anyone worth talking to for more then a couple of minutes. Then they bought me this bicycle four years ago for my birthday, and I've been out almost every night ever since."

"The birth of a swinger," said Sunny's mom. "Maybe I should get one of those for Mickey."

"The phone rings more times for me than it does for them," said Stephan. "And they're teenagers. Well, two of them are. Heidi is into her twenties now."

"Well, good for you," said Sunny's mom. "You make me feel young just looking at you on that thing. In fact, Sunny, go get us some dessert. I've just done my exercising for the week."

Everybody laughed, then Stephan said goodbye and moved along and we went back to our coffee. A few other people came by and said hello and hi and asked Sunny how she was doing. Mrs. Taylor had something to say to all of them.

We stayed there for about two hours, just talking and watching people and drinking our coffee. Sunny and her mom split a piece of carrot cake.

The whole time I was there I felt like I was in another part of the world, or, at least, on a vacation, because the only time I ever did anything like this with Mom and Dad was when we were away somewhere, like in the mountains, or the time we went to Seattle for a conference Dad was at.

Those are the only times I can remember just sitting and actually doing nothing with my parents.

When it was time for me to go home, Sunny asked if I wanted to meet again tomorrow and I said absolutely, so we decided to meet at the library again at noon. Then they walked me to my bus stop and we said goodbye and Sunny and I waited and waited until her mom moved a few steps away so we could kiss again.

On my way home I thought over and over again about everything we had done and how much fun it had been.

The entire bus ride home seemed to be over in about five minutes.

< 10 >

Sunny and I spent every day of the rest of the week together, but on the weekend she had to help plan her Auntie Mavis's birthday party and I had to help Mom and Dad around the house.

It was Lawn & Home Beautification time again: meaning mowing, weeding, trimming, planting, fertilizing, and watering on the outside, and sorting, cleaning, dusting, vacuuming, polishing, washing, and scrubbing on the inside. You can imagine how excited I was about the whole thing, especially after Sunny phoned me at eight o'clock Saturday morning to ask if I wanted to meet them for breakfast and help plan the party.

"I mean, what the heck," she said. "My cousin Theresa always brings her boyfriends along to these family things. Sometimes even two of them show up. That was so funny when that happened one time. You should have seen her beautiful, manicured face. It almost fell off in one big clump right on to her plate. Like a mask. Anyway, we're going to Sam's.

They have the best eggs Benedict in the world. Then we're going to my uncle's house. My rich uncle. He lives by the zoo. He has a pool in his backyard. One night last summer we turned all the lights off and went skinny-dipping. Just the kids. The adults were all inside."

I asked Mom if I could go and she said no. I knew she was going to say that, but it made me feel lousy anyway. Probably because of the way she said it. Not "No, I'm afraid not," or "No, not until you've helped around here, you can meet them in the afternoon." Just no. N-O. Period. Then she handed me a bucket and a rag and told me to help Dad with the windows outside.

Mom's mood had been pretty rotten all week, actually. I didn't know if it had to do with her problems at work or with my brother William and his wife Jennifer or what, but all week she'd been snapping at me and telling me to do this and do that. Then, at the end of the day, she'd forget about everything she'd asked me to do and sit in front of the television, which was pretty strange. Mom is not a big television fan.

Dad wasn't exactly Mr. Happy-Go-Lucky when I went to help him with the windows either, complaining to me that there was too much soap in the water and that the windows would be streaky if we didn't get all of it off. As if streaky windows were the beginning of the end. Then he asked me how old I was, and wondered if I wasn't a big enough boy to do these sorts of chores on my own, maybe even during the weekdays, since it was summer holidays and I had nothing better to do, so he could tend to more important matters on the weekends. Or, at least, more enjoyable.

As I saw it, this wasn't exactly the kind of stimulating father-son talk you see in the movies all the time, nor was it all that much fun to be around and listen to, so I left him alone on top of his ladder, and Herbie and I went to get the lawnmower out of the shed. Compared to listening to him, the rattle and roar of the lawnmower sounded pretty appealing to me.

I only got about halfway to the shed when I heard a car pull into our driveway. I turned around and saw it was my brother, William. He was driving a little red sports car these days, a convertible with the top down. He had some kind of lousy dance music turned as loud as it could go on the stereo.

Naturally, he was wearing sunglasses and driving gloves. That's something else about William that drives me crazy. Even when he was away from his office and out with his family at our house or at a park for a picnic, it always looked like he had spent twice as much time on himself and his appearance than on anyone else. It was like that's all he cared about. And he always had these men's magazines with him, like *GQ* and *Vanity Fair* and *Esquire*, that he was always looking at.

William shut off his car and stepped onto the driveway and said hi to dad. Then he turned and looked at me and took off his sunglasses. He's a little taller than I am and about twenty pounds heavier. His hair is short and wavy and brown. He had a little beard on his face that looked absolutely ridiculous, in my opinion.

"Aren't you supposed to be holding the ladder there, Sport?"

That's what he called everybody all the time – Sport. Hey, Sport. How are ya, Sport? What's new, Sport? What sport are you playing there, Sport?

It was his way of being chummy.

"You go ahead," I said. I really didn't feel like talking to him.

"I don't think so," he said. Now he was taking his gloves off, one finger at a time, like some kind of tough guy.

"Then let Dad stay up there by himself. I'm going to get the lawnmower out of the shed."

"And if he falls, you'll come around to catch him?"

"How could I do that?" I said. I knew what he was getting at, but I didn't feel like letting him know it.

"Exactly my point," he said, nodding, as if he had just solved the biggest crime in the world. "You're walking away from your responsibility, Harper. Dad is relying on you to hold the ladder and you'd better get over there and do it before something happens."

Now he was speaking to me like some sort of father figure.

"And what are you doing?" I said. I was ticked off all of a sudden. This guy talking to me about walking away from responsibility. I was just walking away from a grumpy old man who I didn't feel like listening to anymore. William was the one walking away from responsibility, except he wasn't even walking from it. He was driving.

"I've come over for a visit," he said.

"That's pretty responsible. Why don't you go see your own family for a visit?"

He didn't like that one very much. He came walking towards me, slowly. I half expected him to put a toothpick in his mouth and start chewing it, the way the guys do in the movies. Except William probably carried around dental floss instead of toothpicks, and I don't think pulling out a roll of floss would have had the same effect.

"What'd ya say there, Sport?" he said, coming to a stop right in front of me.

"You heard me."

He looked me in the eye.

"Remember when we were kids, and I used to pound the crap out of you all the time because you were so mouthy?"

"I remember when I was a kid, and you were a teenager, and you used to pound the crap out of me all the time."

He nodded. I think he missed the point.

"You think it can't happen again?"

I thought about that for a second.

"I think if you were to try fighting someone who was within ten years of your own age it wouldn't happen again."

He gave me a little shove.

"Always the smart guy, hey Harper? Always the guy with the comeback."

"You're the one who came back. I can't get away from this place."

He stood looking at me again. I could smell his breath, he was so close to me. It smelled minty, like Scope, meaning he even used mouthwash when he got ready in the morning. Even when he wasn't really going anywhere.

"Where would you go?" he said. "If you could get out of 'this place ,' as you call it. Where would you go?"

"Today? I'd go into the city."

"What for?"

"To see somebody."

"Who?"

"Who? My dentist. My teeth feel funny. I think they're too straight or something."

"Come on. Who would you go see?"

At first he was being bossy. Now he was just being nosy.

"I have somebody I'd like to go see."

"A girl?"

"I told you already. My dentist."

He ignored me.

"Is it a girl you want to go see?"

I took a deep breath and closed my eyes. If there was one person in the world I didn't feel like telling this to, it was William, but I kind of felt that I had to. Besides, his Scope-breath was starting to get to me.

"Yes. It's a girl."

He stood back and smiled, as if I had impressed him

"A girlfriend?" he said. His eyebrows went straight up.

"No," I said. "A girl poodle. It's my pet-grooming class today and I really don't want to miss out."

"What's her name?"

He wasn't going to let me go until I told him. He wasn't even paying attention to my jokes anymore.

"Sunny," I said.

His face fell into a frown.

"Sunny," he said.

"Yes, as in, 'My, what a sunny day it was until you drove up in your car.'"

I know this wasn't exactly true, but he didn't have to know about it.

"What did Mom have to say about that?"

"She said I could still go out with her as long as Sunny promises to change her name when she turns eighteen."

"I bet. How long have you been seeing her?"

"I met her at a camp I went to. About two weeks, I guess."

"Have Mom and Dad met her?"

"Not yet."

"Better get on it there, Sport. With a name like Sunny, Mom's going to have a lot of ideas floating around in her head. You better do something about that quick. Unless they're true. What kind of a girl is she?"

I rolled my eyes and took another deep breath.

"She lives in a treehouse with her little sister, Rainbow. Their parents live in a canoe on a lake up north."

William smiled and gave me a knock on the shoulder.

"Alright, funny guy. I'll leave you alone. But if ever you need any advice, you call me. I'll be there for you."

I nodded. I was going to say something smart, like, "Thanks, but I'd kind of like this to work out for us," but I didn't.

William wasn't such a bad guy and I knew he was really hurting with everything going on in his life. That's why he was over at the house. He wanted to talk to Mom and Dad.

"Where is Mom, anyway?" he said, walking past me.

He was so casual about it, like he didn't even want me to know that anything was the matter.

I told him she was in the house, then I carried on into the backyard to finally get the lawnmower out of the shed.

< 11 >

After I finished mowing the lawn, I put the lawnmower away and got the trimmer out and did all around the trees and along the edges of the driveway and the patio. Then I got a bucket and the hose and washed Mom's car.

I wasn't sure what was inspiring me to do all this, except that it was a very beautiful day outside and everything was completely quiet and peaceful. Even Herbie was enjoying a little snooze on the deck in the backyard, and he doesn't fall asleep outside very often.

Besides, I knew I wasn't going anywhere, and William was still over, so I figured I knew what they were talking about in the kitchen.

I dried Mom's car and then I went inside to get something to eat. William, Mom and Dad were sitting around the table. Mom looked as if she had been crying. Dad looked very solemn and serious. William just stared at the coffee cup in front of him. He didn't look up at me or anything.

"Anybody want some lunch?" I said, opening the fridge. I thought I should say something.

William and Dad shook their heads.

"You go ahead," said Mom. She looked at me for a second and then looked away.

I decided to make myself a sandwich.

I took my time making it, partly because I wasn't sure what I wanted on it, but also because I wanted to hear at least something that was being said. I mean, William is my brother and I've known his wife Jennifer for about ten years, so it wasn't like I should be cut out from everything.

Finally, after about five minutes, which is a very long time for anybody to make a sandwich, Mom said, "So, what happens now?"

William shrugged his shoulders. He looked completely opposite from the guy who had wheeled into the driveway in his super-hot sports car two hours ago.

"Her lawyer will talk to my lawyer, I guess. I don't know," he said.

"Do you even have a lawyer?" said Mom.

"I've talked with Clarissa," said William. Clarissa is my sister. Her husband is a lawyer.

That was all they said. They fell silent again after that and didn't say another word. Mom closed her eyes and shook her head. I could see her hands were shaking a little. She was having a pretty hard time with this.

So I just said, "I'll be downstairs," and started to leave.

"What did you get done outside, Harper?"

Mom was talking to me now. Her face was streaked with tears and her eyes looked very tired and sad.

I told her everything I'd done. I was suddenly very glad that I'd done it all.

"Wow. Thank you," she said, her mood brightening for a moment.

"Did you get along the side of the house with the trimmer?" said Dad, who had apparently survived his solo act on the ladder.

"Yes, I did," I said.

"Thata boy."

Then William piped up. They all seemed to suddenly appreciate having something else to talk about for a change.

"Hey, did you guys hear? Harper has a girlfriend."

Dad looked at William. I don't think he had heard.

Mom smiled and looked at the Kleenex she had in her hand.

"She's not a girlfriend, William. She's a friend. They met at a writing camp."

"He told me he had a girlfriend."

Mom looked at me. I shrugged my shoulders.

"What's the difference?" I said.

"Hey," said William. "I'll tell you the difference. Have you kissed her?"

"William," said Mom.

I rolled my eyes.

"What?" said William. "He wants to know what the difference is between a friend and a girlfriend. I can ask him that. I'm his brother." Then he turned and asked me again. "Have you kissed her?"

I thought for a moment whether I should answer him or not, and then I said, "Yes. I've kissed her."

What did the guy think I was, a mannequin?

Mom sat back in her chair and rubbed her forehead.

William and Dad looked at each other. They were big men now, preparing to welcome a new kid into their fold.

"On the lips?" said William.

"William, that's enough," said Mom, as if he was seven years old again.

"Yes. On the lips," I said.

"Harper," said Mom.

"That sounds like a girlfriend," said William, pointing his finger to emphasize the point.

Dad turned and looked at me and winked. He had a little smile on his face. I think he kind of felt bad for the way he was with me outside, complaining about everything and all that. He's not usually like that. Actually, he's usually pretty positive, when he's home. But I know he likes doing chores about as much as I do, so he was probably as excited about working around the house as I was. And, I know he's not happy about the things going on in William's life. Dad liked Jennifer and he loved his grandkids.

Mom just looked at me, but didn't say anything. It was almost as if this little act of me kissing a girl was enough to push her right over the edge.

Then she got up from the table and walked over to where I was standing and opened the refrigerator. She reached inside and pulled out a casserole dish and set it on the counter.

Her hands were shaking again when she put it down and she kept closing her eyes and rubbing her forehead. I think she had a headache.

"You okay, Mom?" I said.

She gave a little smile and nodded. There was nothing to the smile. Just her lips doing a little exercise, and not too energetically at that. Then she took a deep breath and pulled out something else from the fridge.

She was obviously thinking about a few things.

"Have you met her folks yet?" said William, from the table.

"Yes, I have," I said.

"What are they like?"

I told him. I said that her dad likes books and playing games like chess and Twenty Questions and has won the In-House Scrabble Tournament at the library two years in a row. Then I told them all about her mom – how she buys good treats for campfires, is so easy to talk to, spends her days padding around their apartment in her slippers or sitting in front of the keyboard at her computer, and loves spending her nights at that little sidewalk cafe talking to anybody and everybody who walks, runs, or rides by.

"Sounds like quite a family," said William. "I remember Jennifer's mom used to love watching baseball. Didn't matter who was playing or what level it was. She'd take her lawn chair across the street to watch the kids and she had season tickets to the Trappers games. She had a big satellite dish on the roof so she could pick up the Blue Jays or

Expos wherever they were playing. I didn't know a thing about baseball until I sat down and watched a game with her one time. Then I felt like I knew everything. She even had a t.v in her hospital room."

"Sunny has a brother who likes baseball," I said. Then I told William all about Mickey.

William took another sip from his coffee, then he said, "So, you're spending a lot of time over there?"

"Every day this week," I said. I was smiling when I said it, thinking about all the fun things Sunny and I had done, which still did not include making out on her couch, since Mrs. Taylor was home all the time. "It's fun, you know. Doing different things. Going to the park. Sitting on their balcony. Reading magazines. They have a ton of magazines over there. And Sunny knows where all these secondhand bookstores are. Are they ever fun to go into. And you can walk in with two dollars in your pocket and leave with about three books and some change."

"They live in the city?"

"Yeah, in this cool little apartment. It's not really little, but it's a lot smaller than our house. We hang out there and rent movies in the middle of the day. Sunny's mom even asked me to help her with some work she's doing. She's trying to write something for this magazine. She asked me to help her out."

William nodded. You could tell he was impressed, although I'm not sure which part impressed him the most – the apartment or the bookstores or just the fact that I had a girlfriend.

Dad was just sitting there. I think his mind had

already switched on to something else. Or maybe he was remembering the good old days when he was dating Mom, assuming they were good old days.

Then he stood up and excused himself and said he had to have a shower before he went out to the grand opening of a new business in town. A ribbon-cutting, I think they call it.

"It's that new Tire Center in the Industrial Park. Quite a nice place, actually. I think they'll do okay," he said, as if he actually believed that we were all very interested in what kind of a new business was opening. I mean, at the moment, Mom and William could not have cared less, and for me, I'm pretty well like that all the time.

"Wish them luck for me," I said. I was being a little bit smart and Dad gave me a look, but it wasn't a bad look or anything. Just a look that said he heard me.

That's one of the things town councillors have to do sometimes – make appearances at things like grand openings and town-wide barbecues and any kind of festival that may be going on. Dad has been going to these things for years and he always looks so happy and proud to be there when you see his picture in the paper, even though, especially on days like today, he must have other things on his mind.

He looked at Mom when he went by, but he didn't say anything. I really don't know how much the two of them have talked about William's separation, or even Mom's problems at work. I really don't even know how much the two of them talk at all. They're almost never home together, and when they go out, it's usually to parties or banquets or things like that where it's pretty hard for two people to sit down and work something through. And I don't think they have ever had a personal conversation in front of me. That's just not something they do. It's like they have no problem reminding me (every day) that they are my parents, but when it comes to their husband-and-wife side, they'd just as soon keep that a secret. Even from each other, apparently.

So, Dad left the kitchen to have a shower and Mom didn't even look in his direction or say anything to him. She was busy getting some food ready to eat. I guess everybody was hungry, all of a sudden.

She was moving all over the kitchen, pulling plates from the cupboard and ketchup from the fridge. She was making a fair bit of noise, too, actually. She's usually pretty careful with things like plates.

"You need a hand there, Mom?" I said, taking a break from my stories about Sunny.

"Oh, no, I'm fine," she said, in a voice that didn't sound particularly good. "You two just keep on talking. I'm enjoying listening to how much fun the two of you have when you're out of the house. Come over here when you have problems, but go away when you want to put your feet up and relax."

She was upset again. I knew I shouldn't have said anything to William.

"Mom, what can I say?" I said, feeling the need to explain myself further. "Mr. and Mrs. Taylor are different, that's all. They don't work all the time. Mrs. Taylor doesn't run around the house with a toothbrush in her mouth and the vacuum cleaner in her hand so she can get done two things at once. She doesn't care if we sit and watch movies all afternoon. She joins us half the time. It's the summer. School's out for a couple of months."

I wasn't saying it as a criticism, but Mom was sure taking it as one.

She pulled a dish out of the microwave and banged it on the counter. Then she put something else in and slammed the door and punched in the time and hit the start button like she was trying to poke a hole through it.

"Well, Harper," she said, staring at the numbers on the oven, which was just fine with me, because her eyes were glowing with more heat than the microwaves in the stupid thing. "I'm glad you've finally found a mother you can have some real fun with. I know you've been looking for quite some time now."

"Mom –" I said, not sure of what I would say next. Not that it mattered.

"Now, if you'll excuse me, I have to get your father some lunch, so he won't be late for his whatever-the hell-it-is he's going to this afternoon, and your brother has to eat and be on his way. I hope you won't mind me feeding two people at once. Unless you consider that to be doing two things at once as well. I hope you don't have a problem with that."

She was banging and clanging around the kitchen again. Her hands were really shaking when she poured Dad a glass of milk. Then she put the glass in the refrigerator and left the milk jug on the counter, which I knew was a mistake.

"Your brother's life is falling apart. I never hear from your sister. She could be living on the moon right now and I wouldn't know about it. And now you're off slumming at some girl's house you're too afraid to let us meet. You know, I was serious the other day when I said I wanted to meet her. When I was driving you home from camp? That boring writing camp your father and I sent you to. And paid for. It was all my idea, by the way. Your own miserable mom thought of that. I thought you might enjoy something like that. Little did I know you would use it to get at least one foot out the door."

I rolled my eyes. This was starting to get a bit heavy for me, not to mention dramatic.

"I think you're getting a little carried away there, Mom," I said. I mean, what, I actually planned to meet somebody at that camp?

"Oh, you do, do you?" she said, her voice starting to go way up. She was looking for something on the counter. "Well, isn't that a shame. Poor little Harper thinks I'm getting carried away again. Well, boo-hoo. Too bad. Now where's the milk? Where's the damn glass of milk I poured for your father?"

"It's in the fridge," I said. I was just standing there beside her. I didn't want to go get it.

"It's not in the fridge. It was right here on the counter. Now, where is it?"

"You put it in the fridge by mistake," I said. I wasn't even looking at her when I was talking.

She was really in a wild mood.

She swung open the fridge door and looked and saw the milk. Then she grabbed it and pulled it out so fast that it spilled all over her arm and down on to the floor. She stopped moving. She just stood there and looked at her arm and then down at the floor. Then she shoved the glass at me and said, "Give that to your father," and left the kitchen.

I turned around and looked at William. He looked at me, then he took a great, big, deep breath and let it out very slowly and stared at the table.

I walked over and put the milk down.

"Mom is going through a lot right now," he said, quietly.

"I can see that," I said, even though I really couldn't. Not all of it, anyway.

"Her grandchildren are moving to Ontario and her little baby is in love with another woman," he said, summing it all up.

I don't know which part surprised me more, that William's wife Jennifer was taking the kids to her parents' house in Ottawa, or that he knew I was in love. And since when was I in love with Mom?

"What?" I said. I know it wasn't much of a response, but it somehow summed up how I was feeling.

"Jennifer's going back home for a while. She's taking the kids with her. She wants a divorce. And you," he said, pointing his finger at me, "you're stepping out. You're getting ready to leave the nest. I'm flying back in and you're flying out."

"You're moving back in with Mom and Dad?" I said. I had to take care of that little piece of information before I could move on.

"Not literally," he said. "But I've been spending more time here than I have in about the last fifteen years, in case you haven't noticed."

"I've noticed," I said. I felt kind of bad for reacting the way I did. I think I came off sounding like he had just said, "The whole place is contaminated, and anyone living here is contaminated, too." Which really is not too far from the truth, when you think about it. At least, that's how I feel on days like this.

We were both quiet for a minute, then I said, "Does she actually think that I'm getting ready to move out?"

William shook his head.

"No. I doubt it. But for the first time ever, there's another woman in your life besides her, and to her, that means she's losing you. I went through the same thing with her. Except I was the first one in the family to do it. I was the one who brought someone home for the first time, and you know what I did? I kissed her right in front of Mom and Dad. I wanted to show them that my love for this girl was real. I was sixteen years old. All three of them just about went right through the roof. Mom, Dad, and Raquel, or Rachel, or whoever she was. I kissed her right here in the kitchen. They were standing right where you are now. I'll never forget that. The look on Mom's face. She told me later that she had been ready to tear Rachel's hair out. Or whatever her name was. Mom figured she had put me up to it."

"How long did it take her to cool down?"

"We never went out again," said William. "I think I scared her. I think she thought, 'If this guy's kissing me in front of his parents, what's he going to be like when we're alone?'"

"I mean Mom," I said. "How long did it take Mom to cool down?"

"Oh. I don't know. Not too long. Couple days. But she's got a lot more on her mind now. I don't know how long this will take."

That didn't make me feel any better.

I looked at William and then I looked away. This was the closest thing to a brother-to-brother chat we'd ever had in our lives, and it was coming at about the worst time. Or at least, it felt like the worst time, all of a sudden.

< 12 >

On Sunday, I invited Sunny over to the house for supper. I just woke up in the morning and picked up the phone in my bedroom and said, "How would you like to have supper at my place tonight?" She said sure in about half a second. I guess it was something she had been thinking about, meeting my parents and seeing where I live and all that.

I didn't tell her anything about what had happened the day before, or about Mom going on about "Still not knowing what your girlfriend looks like," or whatever it was she said. I just said, "Great. Why don't you come over around five o'clock?" and I gave her my address.

Then she asked me about the kind of flowers Mom liked and whether Mom would be offended if she brought dessert.

I told her roses, which was a guess, because I don't think I had ever bought Mom flowers before, and no, Mom would not be offended, even though I hadn't really thought about it. How could anyone be offended if someone else brings them dessert?

"Okay," said Sunny, as if she was taking my order over the phone. "Roses and dessert. Perfect. I'll see you at five o'clock." Then we hung up.

I went downstairs to tell Mom and Dad. I wasn't nervous or anything. Even after yesterday, I knew they would be excited about finally getting a chance to meet Sunny. Especially Mom.

They were sitting in the kitchen. Dad was reading the newspaper. Mom was just sitting there looking out the window. She had a mug of coffee in her hands. She looked pretty tired. Actually, she looked pretty awful.

"Mom," I said. She looked at me. I cleared my throat. She did not look like she was in the mood for excitement.

"What?" she said. Her voice was very flat and tired and did not exactly sound interested in what I had to say. And she didn't say, "What is it, dear?" or "Yes, honey?" or even, "Yes?" in kind of a pleasant way. She just said, "What?" and I started to think right then that maybe this wasn't such a terrific idea after all, trying to cheer her up by inviting Sunny over to her house. Maybe I should have just volunteered to polish the door handles or something.

"Uhm," I said. I cleared my throat again, even though I didn't have a cold. I thought about calling Sunny back, but I remembered how excited and happy she was. Then I thought about lying to her, and telling her Mom was sick with the flu, or Dad hurt his foot falling off the ladder. That didn't stick either.

So I took a deep breath and said my piece.

"I've invited Sunny over for supper tonight."

Mom blinked a couple of times and continued to stare at me. Dad lowered the paper he was reading so I could just see his eyes over the page. Mom took another sip of her coffee.

"What are you making?" she said, finally, after about a minute of complete silence.

I looked at her.

"What am *I* making?" I said.

"Yes," said Mom.

"I was kind of hoping you would make something," I said, which was the truth.

She continued to stare at me. Her eyes showed no emotion at all.

"Are you going to clean the house?"

I looked around me. Everything looked pretty immaculate, but I take after Dad in the cleanliness department, so you never know.

"Sure," I said, shrugging my shoulders. I did see a magazine on the kitchen counter that I could put away, and I figured their coffee cups could go in the dishwasher.

Everything was quiet again after that, then Dad lowered the newspaper from in front of his face and said, "We could have a barbecue." I looked at him with tremendous relief. He was coming to my rescue. I could practically hear his white horse as it galloped towards me. "In the backyard," he went on. "Harper did all that work in the yard yesterday. We could sit outside and enjoy the deck."

"Yes," I said, my eyes lighting up. If I was eighteen years old, I would have voted for him right there on the spot. Even without an election going on. "We could have a barbecue in the backyard. Then Dad could do all the work and you could just sit and talk with Sunny."

Dad gave me a look, but in general, his looks were nothing like Mom's.

I was very hopeful now. Things were suddenly coming together.

But Mom was still just sitting there, and she still did not look too terribly interested in entertaining anyone.

I guess my timing was a bit off. Then I remembered something.

"You don't have to worry about dessert, either. Sunny's bringing it."

Mom took a deep breath.

"That's very kind of her," she said.

"I know," I said, proudly, as if to say, "That's my Sunny." Then I said, "And she's bringing flowers, too. Red roses."

Mom started to brighten a bit.

"Really? How thoughtful of her."

"That's what I said," I said, even though I hadn't.

"It sounds to me like you two men could learn a lot from this young lady. I should invite William over to meet her, too."

The smile dropped from my face.

"You're joking, right? About William?"

I mean, our nice little brother-to-brother chat aside, I'd still rather have to call long distance to get a hold of the guy.

"Yes," said Mom, "but not about the other part."

She took another sip of coffee and put her cup down on the table. Then she stood up.

"Well, I guess I should start to get ready then. Heaven knows how long it will take me to look good today. You boys plan the menu and do whatever shopping you have to do. Leave yourselves plenty of time to do the cooking. And you know I like a big salad. I'll be upstairs."

She walked past me and smiled. I think she was starting to feel a bit better.

I looked at Dad. It felt good knowing that he had been there for me, or at least, that's how I saw it.

I wanted to say thanks, but instead I said, "What was it like the first time you brought Mom home to your Mom and Dad's house?"

I felt like talking with him a little, before we got going.

He smiled. "The first time I brought your mother to my house, Dad was changing a tire on the car in the driveway. She walked up to him and said, 'Hello, Mr. Winslow,' and he grunted something. Then he stood up and dusted off his hands and said, 'That boy of mine lent the car to someone last night and they drove too close to the curb. Just about popped the tire in two.' Your mother's face went pure red. She said, 'I didn't know that happened.' Dad said, 'Well, it did, and if I ever meet this Alex person, I'm gonna let him know about it. He owes me a new tire.' We didn't tell him for ten years that Alex was your mother's middle name, Alexandra. She used to go by that. I had taken her out driving the night before. She had never driven a car before. I knew she'd bumped the curb, but I never knew she'd hit it that hard. Neither did she. She felt so bad about it. Ten years later she walked up to Dad and said, 'Mr. Winslow, there's something I have to tell you,' and she rolled this shiny new radial tire towards him. His eyes just about popped right out of his head. I don't think he ever believed that she was Alex."

I was laughing when Dad finished his story. It made me feel pretty good, you know, hearing a story from him that had nothing to do with being a parent or a politician or a doctor.

Then he said, "Well, come on, kid. We have some work to do," and got up from the table. "I wonder what stories Mom is going to have about you tonight," he added. I looked at him. All of a sudden, I remembered why I hadn't invited Sunny to the house earlier.

"She's probably up there planning them all right now," he said, starting to laugh. "I can think of a few gems myself."

He looked at me. He looked so happy.

It's a good thing one of us did, I guess.

< 13 >

At five-fifteen the doorbell rang. I opened the door and Sunny was standing there with a bouquet of roses in one hand and a pie in the other. She was wearing a light blue sundress and sand-colored sandals. She looked absolutely gorgeous.

"Hi," she said, standing there with this super-big smile on her face. "I just travelled from Edmonton to Emville on a bus with these two things in my hands. Can you believe it? And not one person asked me where I was going or what I was doing with them."

I just looked at her for a minute, drinking her in from head to toe, as I read in a book somewhere, and invited her in.

"Nice place," she said, looking around.

"I do what I can," I said, with a shrug. Then I took the pie and the roses.

"So, how are you?" she said. She was very re-laxed. "Don't I get a kiss?"

I looked at her. I was not very relaxed. I was in high-stress mode, actually: the better Mom had started to feel throughout the day, the more worried I got, and at four-thirty, when she came downstairs beaming like a patio lantern and gave me a hug and said, "Harper, you've done the right thing, inviting Sunny over to the house tonight. Thank you. I can't wait to meet her," I had to run into the bathroom and relieve myself.

I read almost an entire *People* magazine, I was in there so long. My stomach just would not settle down.

Besides, I remembered the story William had told me about kissing his first girlfriend in front of Mom and Dad.

"How about after?" I said. If there was an after.

"How about now?" said Sunny, and she came towards me and gave me a kiss right on my lips. Not a particularly short kiss, either, and because I was holding a pie in one hand and roses in the other, I could hardly defend myself.

Then I heard a sound behind me.

"Ahem," said Mom. "You two lovebirds save that until the old people have gone to bed."

She was laughing when she said it, thank goodness. Then she said, "You must be Sunny. Hi. I'm Harper's mom. Mrs. Winslow."

She held out her hand.

Sunny smiled and laughed and said, without missing a beat, as if she had just been showing me a new button on her dress, "You look like his sister. Hi. It's wonderful to meet you. These are for you." She pointed to the flowers and pie I had in my hands.

Mom was naturally flattered by all of this. She

invited Sunny in and told me to put the pie in the oven and the roses in a vase, as if she believed that if she didn't say anything, I might put the flowers in the oven and the pie in a vase, which, given my condition at the time, was probably not so far out of the question.

Dad was outside cooking chicken on the barbecue. I heard his cheery "Hello!" from where I was standing. I went into the kitchen to find a vase. I saw the three of them standing on the deck, pointing to different things in the backyard – the trees, the flowers, the gazebo – we had it all. Sunny showed amazing interest in everything Mom and Dad told her, then Mom invited her to sit down on one of the lawn chairs and asked what she would like to drink.

"I'll have a little glass of wine," said Sunny, holding her thumb and index finger about an inch apart. "If that's alright with you. Mom and Dad said I could have a little glass of wine tonight, since it's such a special occasion."

My jaw thunked against the counter in the kitchen and sprang back up and rattled the top row of my teeth. *Why did she have to say wine? Now Mom and Dad would think all we did was sit around her place in the afternoon sucking booze out of bottles in brown paper bags.*

"What a wonderful idea," said Mom, who I know had been thinking more along the lines of grape juice or pop. "Ben, we have some wine chilling in the fridge, don't we? Some white wine? I prefer white. What do you like, Sunny?"

"White is fine. I like red with spaghetti. Don't ask me why. It's just whenever we have spaghetti, I like to have a little glass of red wine with it. If we have any in the house. My mom and dad are not big wine drinkers."

I rolled my eyes and leaned heavily on the kitchen counter. *My girlfriend drinks enough wine to know what types she likes with certain meals, and she's telling my parents about it.*

"Harper never drinks wine," said Mom. "We've offered it to him. I think he had it once and he threw up."

Sunny let out a snort and started to laugh.

I decided to go outside.

"I prefer beer," I said, by way of announcing myself. "By the case. I drink it late at night watching re-runs of "Married With Children" and "Charlie's Angels". I find I get so much more out of them the second and third times around. And I didn't throw up, Mom. I spit it out because it tasted so lousy. I didn't throw it up."

"Well, you certainly made enough racket," said Mom, as Dad stepped around me to get the wine from the house. "You know, Harper has always been like that," she added, turning back to Sunny. "When he's sick, everyone in the house has to know about it. 'I'm gonna be sick! Look out! I'm gonna throw up!' He has to run around the house saying this before he gets to the toilet. Fortunately, he always gets there in time. Usually. I shouldn't say always."

They talked on. I waited patiently for Mom to bring up my bowel movements as a topic of conversation, or the time I was constipated after eating too much cheese, or whatever it was that brought out the Metamucil from the cupboard above the bathtub in the bathroom.

Dad finally came out with their wine. Then he tapped me on the shoulder and handed me a beer.

"Here you go, Sport," he said, quoting William. "I understand this is your preference."

I looked at him, then at the bottle of beer that was practically hanging in my face, then back at him again.

"You want that with a glass?" he said. He had this big grin on his face. I took the beer from him. This was the first beer Dad had ever given me.

"My, my," said Mom, looking at me. I felt like a little kid who had just been given a third cookie. "This *is* a special occasion."

"To Harper and Sunny," said Dad, holding his beer in the air.

"To first love," said Mom, clinking glasses with Sunny.

I didn't clink my glass with anybody. I was still trying to figure out who these people were.

"I didn't know I was your first love," said Sunny, after taking a sip of her wine.

"Of course you are," said Mom, raising her glass to her mouth, before I could say anything.

"You told me you've made out with someone before. On a couch. Remember? After I lost my contact lens?"

I froze. Mom jerked forward and almost spit out the wine she had just taken in. Dad's eyebrows shot up to the second floor of our house. I looked for somewhere to hide and remembered the beer I had in my hand, so I lifted it to my mouth, closed my eyes, and drank to escape.

I don't know if Sunny said this to be funny, or to embarrass me, or because she didn't think it was a big deal – talking about kissing in front of my parents – but I can tell you, it felt like a big deal at the moment.

"Harper?" said Mom, as soon as she recovered. "On a couch?" She had a Kleenex out and was dabbing her mouth with it. She was also laughing pretty hard. "On our couch?"

"That's what he said," said Sunny. "Isn't that what you said?" She looked back at me.

I brought the beer down from my mouth and swallowed hard. I took this to be one of those situations that life threw at you once in awhile, and I knew that the way I dealt with it would have an enormous impact on my future, or at least, on whether or not I would ever see Sunny again, or anyone else outside of my immediate family.

"I think so," I said, my eyes starting to bulge from my head. I'm not exactly a seasoned beer drinker. "I was just making it up."

"Were you?" said Sunny. She seemed genuinely surprised, and a little disappointed, for some reason.

"I don't think Harper has ever made out with anyone on a couch before," said Mom, shaking her head. She was now dabbing at the tears in her eyes.

"We were rolling around on the grass," I said. "On a hot summer night."

That made them quiet for a minute.

Sunny looked at me and narrowed her eyes, like she was trying to decide whether I was joking or not. Mom looked at me and took another sip of her wine. Dad stood up and lifted the lid of the barbecue and said, "Chicken's ready. Who would like sour cream on their baked potato?"

I brought all the condiments out on a tray and set them down on a side table we have next to the custom-built picnic table William made when he was in Industrial Arts in high school. It was a very nice table that needed only two skinny little novels under each leg on one side to make it level.

While I was inside the kitchen, I saw Dad casually slip over to my chair and take my beer away. I guess that was his way of saying that I had had enough, that one more sip and I might pour salad dressing on my chicken, or something reckless like that, and be unfit to deal with the consequences.

We enjoyed a pleasant dinner together. Mom asked Dad four thousand times if he was sure the chicken was done, and commented again on the fact that he did not buy the ultra-low-fat salad dressing, but the regular kind instead, which, to hear her talk, could clog your veins faster than a roadblock could stop traffic.

Then she asked Sunny who did the cooking at her place.

"We all do," said Sunny. "Mom usually makes breakfast because she's always the first one up. She can't sleep late, for some reason. She has afternoon naps all the time and stays up late every night, but she can't sleep in. Not even past seven o'clock. To her, that is sleeping in. That's how I am, for the most part. Although every once in awhile I can sleep to, like, ten o'clock, if I'm really tired. My brother, Mickey, and my dad, they can sleep through anything. You really have to make some noise to wake them up, especially Mickey. Then again, my dad's always up early, too. Probably because morning is his favorite time of day.

"Anyway, Mickey and I usually make lunch. Sandwiches or soup or something like that. Mickey likes waffles. Then for supper, it's whoever wants to make it. Sometimes it's my dad, my mom, Mickey, me."

"What does your father do?" said Dad. This was his favorite question, too, as well as Mom's.

Mom immediately started to laugh, and nearly choked again on a bite of something she had just put in her mouth.

"Excuse me," she said. She turned to Sunny. "Did Harper ever tell you what he said to me when I asked him that question?"

My face turned deep red again, for the thirteenth time in the last half-hour. Was there nothing that I had said or done in the first sixteen years of my life that was not going to be discussed tonight?

"No," said Sunny, looking at me, then back at Mom.

"I asked him that question on our way home from camp, he was talking all about you, very flattering by the way, and of course, I can see why. But anyway, I asked him that, I said, 'What does her father do?' because you know, I wanted to know, and he said, in that wonderful deadpan humor of his, 'He's a stripper.'"

Mom broke out in another wild fit of laughter after that.

"I hope I'm not thinking about that when I'm introduced to him," she said, barely getting it all out, she was laughing so hard. I'm sure the wine she was drinking had something to do with it. She was well into her second glass.

I hope it did, anyway.

The thing was, she was the only one who found the joke to be funny. Sunny just looked at her, then at me, and mouthed the words, "A stripper?" and raised her eyebrows.

I shrugged my shoulders. I wanted to explain to her the context in which the original joke had been made, but of course, that was obviously impossible.

Then Dad said, "I guess we'll leave that one alone for a while. More salad anyone? Corn? Come on, Sunny. There's lots here."

"My dad works in a library," said Sunny, finally. "He's a reference librarian downtown."

"Is that right?" said Dad, who then engaged with Sunny in a very fascinating discussion about library systems today, and the importance of exposing everyone in our society to books and so on, regardless of their financial standing.

By the end of their conversation, I'm sure she was ready to vote for him, too.

After supper, we had Sunny's apple pie, which was delicious, and coffee.

I poured myself a cup and added some cream and sugar. Mom watched me closely and when I was done and sitting down again, she said, "You see, Harper, this is one of the reasons why I was so upset yesterday. You're growing up. You're growing away from us."

I thought this comment was a bit heavy for the evening, but naturally, Sunny picked up on it and her and Mom started up this massive conversation about parents giving their kids room to grow and how difficult it can be sometimes. Then Mom started in about William. Dad moved his chair over so he was closer to them and could talk in a nice low voice so that if any of the neighbors were crouched by their fences eavesdropping, they wouldn't hear anything.

I just kept looking at Sunny as she talked away and thought about how much I wanted to be alone with her. I wanted this night to end so we could meet somewhere tomorrow and go to a park and really roll around in the grass.

Then I heard Mom say to her, "Anyway, I don't suppose your parents are too caught up in any of this stuff yet. You and your brother are still a bit young to be putting them through a divorce and child custody and that sort of thing."

"Yes," said Sunny, nodding, "but we have an issue or two to deal with. I have a chance to go to Toronto this fall to an art school and my mom does not want me to go. She says it's because you don't have to go to Toronto to be an artist, which I already know, but I think it's because she doesn't want me to leave home. Even though I'd be living with family, my dad's sister, who my mom hates, by the way, she does not want me to go. Dad says it's up to me. Mom's not quite there yet."

"Harper never told me about this," said Mom, who didn't even look at me when she said it, as if I wasn't there anymore.

"No, he hasn't," said Dad, who didn't even know about Sunny until twenty-four hours ago.

"Oh, yes," said Sunny, and she told Mom and Dad all about her Auntie Babs' invitation to an art school in Toronto, and about the beautiful place her aunt lives in, right there in the middle of it all on Yonge Street, and about her aunt's beautiful bakery.

By the time she stopped talking, I felt thoroughly sick.

"So, I don't know if I'm going or not," said Sunny, to wrap it up. "There's a few unknowns out there to deal with yet." I'm sure she was talking about her Auntie Mavis, and me, hopefully.

"Oh, you must go," said Mom. This was the beginning of her Women-Be-Proud spiel. "It's a chance to travel and meet new people. New influences. It doesn't matter if it's Toronto you go to or Regina or New York City. It's an opportunity to go out and do something different. Look what going to that little writing camp did for Harper. It's changed his life. He's a different person."

"It's just a cup of coffee, Mom," I said, partly for levity, and partly to shut her up. I mean, if I was a different person, it was because I had met Sunny. So what was Mom doing encouraging her to take a hike for a year on the other side of the country?

"I know," said Sunny. She looked at me and smiled. I tried to smile back but I couldn't, so I gave her a little fake smile, which basically said, "Thanks so much for bringing all this up, and I'm delighted to hear you're still thinking about going."

"I'll have to decide soon," Sunny went on. "Before the end of the summer."

Mom looked at Sunny and said, "You'll make the right decision. You go to that art school and come back here and paint pictures while Harper writes his books. One year isn't a long time. Not when you're your age."

Sunny smiled and said, "Thanks," then she looked over at me, but I didn't feel like looking at her, so I stared off over the neighbor's fence instead.

I know I was probably feeling a little bit sorry for myself, but I was also very scared about losing her.

Mom and Dad started carting some of the things from supper into the house. Sunny offered to help, but Mom told her to stay put and enjoy the fresh air.

"But no smooching," she added. "Remember, this is Emville. You only do that sort of thing inside or it'll be all over town."

Sunny laughed, and then, when Mom went inside, she moved her chair over beside mine and leaned over and gave me a big kiss again, right on the lips. This one had some passion to it, as if she had been sitting there all this time thinking about the same kinds of things that I had been thinking about before she got into the Toronto thing.

In about three seconds I had forgotten I was mad at her.

We walked over to the gazebo and made out like crazy until Dad called out to see if Sunny was ready for a ride home. I didn't want to let her go, but I pretty well had to, so I made like I was giving her a tour of the backyard, and began talking really loudly about the peonies over here that Mom planted and where Dad had bought the gazebo, and we made our way back to the house.

We were giggling and laughing like crazy, and Sunny's dress looked like it had been crumpled up in a bag for a month.

Then Dad and I gave her a ride home. I was pretty quiet on the way back. So was Dad, for some reason. I don't know what he was thinking about, but I sure knew what I was.

< 14 >

A week later I went to Sunny's Auntie Mavis's birth-day party.

Mom didn't think it was such a great idea for me to go. She said that I would be doing no one any favors if I walked in there and fainted, which was a definite possibility, since I was not exactly a pillar of strength when it came to human suffering.

"You remember the time your brother had the flu?" she said, stating her case. "You were eleven years old and your brother was here for supper and he had the stomach flu and he threw up. You were scared for a week to go into the bathroom upstairs. You had nightmares. Over the stomach flu. And now you want to go visit a person you've never met, who will forget she ever met you the moment you leave her side, who is dying of cancer, because you want to impress your girlfriend?"

She was wrong, of course. I wasn't going for that reason at all, although I couldn't pinpoint ex-actly what the real reason was.

"This woman is going to be lying in a bed with a drip going into her arm. She may or may not be awake. She is going to be in a lot of pain," said Mom, going on, and on. She was in one of her moods again. I think old Gladys, Mom's assistant at the store, was being an even bigger headache than usual, and she had talked with William earlier in the day, which was never a good thing, especially lately.

"She's living at home, Mom. She's not in a hospital," I said.

"Home is the hospital these days. Don't you read the paper? Everyone's at home. If you're not in for an operation, you're at home. There's nothing they can do for her in a hospital."

She was working herself into quite a little rage again. There was not one sign of the happy-go-lucky-woman-sipping-wine-with-her-son's-girlfriend-on-the-deck of a week ago.

Nevertheless, I kept moving towards getting out the door. I buttoned my shirt and put another dab of gel in my hair to make it curly. But I had to admit, I was starting to feel a little sick. Mom wasn't exactly pumping me full of strength and courage with everything she was saying, and I knew she knew what she was talking about.

"You don't think I know these things?" she said, moving through the living room with her feather duster. "I've buried all four of your grandparents, sonny boy, and every one of them was the same. It's a horrible experience, and I have no idea why you're not listening to me. I have no idea why you're doing this."

"You just said it was because I wanted to impress Sunny," I said. Now I was feeling sick and confused.

"Well, you must really like her if that's the reason," said Mom, who already knew I really liked her. She really liked Sunny, too. She had told me about a thousand times. "You must really have a thing for her if that's why you're doing this."

Maybe that was it, I thought to myself.

I felt good thinking about that. Maybe that was the reason.

"She asked me to go," I said, not wanting to get all mushy, especially with the way Mom was at the moment. "What kind of a guy would say no to that?"

Mom stopped dusting and looked at me. She took a deep breath and let it out.

"I'm just trying to protect you, okay, Harper? Sunny is over the shock of seeing her aunt sick. She's used to her now. She's seen her lose weight. Maybe she's seen her lose her hair. But you, you have never seen this woman before, and Sunny's aunt, however good and strong she might be feeling, is going to look different than anyone you have ever seen. So be ready for it. That's all I'm going to say. Be ready for it."

I finished getting dressed and fiddling with my hair and went to open the front door.

"This is a very kind gesture you're doing, Harper," said Mom. I guess she was coming around a little. "I just hope that's all it is."

"So do I," I said back, and went on my way.

I took the bus to Sunny's apartment and rode

with her and her family in their van to her Uncle Stewart's house, where the party was being held. When we walked inside, I saw about thirty people, all standing and sitting, laughing and sipping drinks or eating crackers with some kind of spread on top.

There were streamers all over the place and a huge banner at one end of the room.

I was so nervous I could barely smile, and in the van on the way over I stared out the window so much Sunny started to nudge me with her elbow and ask, "Hey, are you alright?" and "What's the matter? You got bad breath or what?"

I didn't want to tell her that, thanks to Mom, I was absolutely terrified of seeing her aunt.

Sunny and Mickey, of course, were as calm and good-natured as ever, and their mom and dad were chatting away in the front seat of the van as if we were all just going to a movie.

At her uncle's house, Sunny took me by the arm and led me from one relative to the next. It was pretty tough to take, actually, saying "Hi," "Nice to meet you, too," "Fine, thanks," and "Yes, I'm sure we'll see each other again sometime," to everyone, and I was just about to suggest a break when Sunny waved to this small woman sitting in a chair and said, "Here he is. This is Harper."

I smiled and extended my hand and said hi. The woman had large, deep brown eyes, like Sunny's, actually, and a soft white hat on her head. She was tanned. She shook my hand and smiled and said hello. Then she asked me to pass her the pack of cigarettes on the little table behind me.

"This is Auntie Mavis," said Sunny, smiling. "Happy birthday, Auntie." She leaned forward and gave her aunt a kiss.

I looked at Sunny and then at the woman and then back at Sunny.

The woman lit her cigarette with a match, and then shook the match weakly until the flame finally went out. Then she dropped it into an ashtray.

"My last remaining bad habit," she said, in a quiet voice and with a smile. "It will be gone soon. Come, sit down." She motioned with her head to the chair beside her and watched me sit down. Sunny sat beside me on the arm of the chair.

"So, how are you feeling, Auntie?" she said.

Her Auntie Mavis smiled slightly and closed her eyes, then she made a face as if to say, "Not bad, not bad."

"I've been better," she said. "I was very sick this morning. I didn't want to get up. Julia gave me a sponge bath in bed. I don't know how she did it. I was in a terrible mood."

"You look great," said Sunny. "Your clothes and your hat."

Her aunt smiled.

"It's the makeup. It's a bronzing agent or something. Makes me look tanned. I wished I had it when I was younger. I look very athletic when I first put it on. Like I've been outside running in the sun all day."

Then she looked at me again.

"So, how are you, Harper?"

She sounded genuinely interested to hear how I was doing.

"Fine, thank you," I said.

"It's nice to finally meet you. Sunny's been talking about you steadily since she came home from that camp. I wasn't sure if I'd see you or not."

"Oh, I was going to get here sooner or later," I said. Then I realized what she had meant.

"And she tells me you're a writer," she said, without missing a beat.

"Yes. Well, sort of. I mean, I write. I write a little bit. No novels or anything like that. Yet. That's where we met, actually. I met Mickey first and then Sunny. At a camp. Mickey's a good writer, too."

"Yes. I know," said her aunt, nodding. "Who are your favorites?"

"Authors, you mean?"

"Yes."

"Well, uhm ..." Of course I couldn't think of anyone. I don't know if I was still nervous or in shock at how easily I was talking with this person who could be dead in a week, but I was drawing a complete blank until I remembered a book that was lying on the floor in my bedroom. It had fallen off a shelf in my closet that morning when I was looking for a shirt.

"I liked *Huckleberry Finn*," I said. I couldn't even remember who wrote it.

Sunny's Aunt Mavis's eyes suddenly lit up like all the candles on her birthday cake.

"Mark Twain?" she said.

"Yes," I said. That was it. That was the guy's name. Mark Twain.

"Oh, Sunny," said her aunt, with a big smile on

her face, "I like this young man."

"I didn't know you liked Mark Twain," said Sunny. "That's my aunt's favorite writer. That's what Mickey reads to her all the time."

"Oh, sure," I said, as if it was common knowledge that I liked Mark Twain.

"Have you read his essays?" said her aunt.

"Uh, no, I haven't," I said, trying to make it sound like, with all of the reading I do, particularly of the work of Mark Twain, that I couldn't recall whether I had read his essays or not.

"How about his letters?"

"I don't think so."

"Oh, you must. That's where he really shines. His books are wonderful, and his short stories, of course, those tall tales of his, but his letters …" She shook her head and smiled. "He has such wit. I like that more than anything else. A good clever wit."

"Yes," I said. "You can't beat that."

We were all quiet for a moment after that, her aunt obviously in deep thought about Mark Twain, Sunny in deep thought about her aunt, and me in deep thought about how I was going to get out of this.

I didn't have a clue what to say. I knew it was a perfect chance for me to jump in with a comment on Twain's terrific characters or his unforgettable humor, but I honestly didn't know anything about the guy. I figured he was funny because most people who have wit are funny, I think. But I didn't know. I really didn't even know that much about *Huckleberry Finn*, other than Mom always called the book a classic, but she isn't exactly someone I would rely on for information on the literary world, except to hear what some of the authors are wearing these days.

But besides all that, I was starting to feel a little bit guilty about getting this woman so excited because she thought we shared favorite writers. I mean, it would have been worse if I had walked in knowing she liked Mark Twain and said, "Hey, I like Mark Twain, too." That would have been a lot worse than anything I was doing right now. But still, mentioning a book because I tripped over it while I looking for a shirt, and having it turn out to be one of her all-time favorites, that wasn't making me feel too particularly good.

"Harper wrote a story about a little boy who had a favorite shirt," said Sunny, breaking the silence. "Maybe he could read it to you sometime. It was wonderful. What was it called again?"

"'The Happy Shirt,'" I said, feeling grateful to Sunny for changing the subject, and very, very important, now that I had written a story that actually had a title. I even had the picture Sunny had drawn for me to go with it.

Her aunt smiled.

"I'd love to hear it. There was a young man visiting the woman across from me the other week who was a writer. I can't remember his name. He showed me one of his books. I started reading it. It was dreadful. Awful. Oh, I had to put it down. When he came back he asked me what I thought. I told him I couldn't finish it. He said, 'Oh yes, my mom's on chemo, too. She gets sick and tired after her treatments.' I said, 'The chemo had nothing to do with it.' I don't know what he thought of that. He's stopped saying hello to me."

"He wasn't Mark Twain?" I said, as a joke.

"He wasn't anything," said her aunt. "He certainly wasn't a writer. I can say those things now. Years ago I would have read the whole book and come up with something good to say about it. That's one of the advantages I have now, I guess. I can say what's on my mind. Not that I didn't before, but now I enjoy it more and worry less about what someone might think."

We talked some more about this and that.

Her aunt asked me if I lived with my parents and what they did for a living. When I told her Dad was a doctor, she just smiled and said, "I bet he works hard." She never let on that she had any hard feelings towards the medical profession … if she did have any hard feelings, that is.

Then everyone gathered together and we sang her "Happy Birthday." A few people had tears in their eyes, including Sunny. I looked at her aunt and she was just sitting there smiling at everyone, even though they were probably all just a blur.

Maybe she looked different without all of her makeup on, but she sure didn't look sick to me. I know people who are supposedly the picture of health who don't look half as good as she did, or who are nowhere near as friendly and fun to talk with as she was. I mean, to hear her say, "That's one of the advantages I have now …" that's not something you hear dying people say very often. I don't hear it very often, that's for sure. I don't even hear it from people who aren't dying.

By the time everyone was finished singing, Sunny's aunt was looking pretty tired. She clapped at the end of the final round of "For She's A Jolly Good Fellow" and then looked around for Julia, her nurse.

I said goodbye to her and shook her hand. She put both her hands over mine and said, "Nice to meet you, Harper. Let's do it again sometime, okay?" I said, "Okay," and waved as Julia took her arm and led her to a bed that was waiting for her at the back of the house. Then everyone went outside and carried on quietly with the celebration.

I went home hopeful that I would see her again. I wanted to read her my story.

< 15 >

Sunny phoned me the next morning at nine o'clock and said that her mom had just left for a day-long writing workshop and her dad was already at work. I asked her about Mickey and she said, "This is the day he goes in with my dad and helps around the library."

I needed no further information. I was showered and dressed in twenty minutes and knocking on Sunny's apartment door an hour later.

She opened it in about three seconds with a smile on her face that could have lit the world. She was wearing her light blue sundress again (I guess she figured out that I liked it) and invited me inside.

Everything was very peaceful and quiet. The patio doors were open that led to their deck. Sunny asked if I wanted to sit outside for a while and have a glass of orange juice. I said no and laid down on their couch.

I wanted to make out with her. I wanted to feel her body and all of its curves and smoothness. I wanted to do things we had never done before.

I gave her my most seductive smile, which made her laugh, and patted the couch beside me.

"Okay, Casanova," she said, and she laid down on the couch. We were both kind of on our sides, to make room for each other, but pretty soon we were so connected that you couldn't tell us apart.

Sunny was absolutely right, of course. Her couch was a far better place for this sort of thing than those crummy chairs in the theater.

After about fifteen minutes of very passionate kissing, I was feeling very brave and excited (not to mention nervous) and began plotting my next move, and how exactly I was going to do it without coming on too strongly, or worse, looking like an idiot.

I started to fumble around with my fingers on the back of her dress in an attempt to somehow find a way in. I thought I was being quite casual about it, maybe even cool or practiced, as if I had done this type of thing before, when she pulled back from our kiss and said, "What are you doing?"

"What?" I said. I was caught off guard by her question.

"What are you doing? What are you doing with your hands? You're pawing me like a bear marking a tree. I've seen that before on a video. That's what you remind me of."

"What?" I said, again. Now I was embarrassed. But I was also thinking, "Why does she always stop in the middle of a kiss to talk like this?"

"What are you doing with your hands? Are you trying to find my bra or what? It's very irritating."

"Irritating?" I said. So much for coming across as a seasoned lover. But I thought "irritating" was going a bit far. I didn't think I was being irritating. I didn't ask her to put the stupid thing on.

"Yes. Irritating. What are you trying to do, take my bra off or give me a massage or what?"

I rolled onto my back, or at least, I tried to, because there was barely enough room on the couch for me to roll over, and stared at the ceiling. My first steps along the long, twisted road of sexual orientation were not going over too well.

Then I closed my eyes. If there was one thing that was starting to bug me about Sunny, it was that she talked too much. Or maybe it was that she talked too much at the wrong times.

"Yes," I said, my eyes still closed. I could not imagine talking about this with them open. "I am trying to take your bra off. Is that okay?"

I shook my head a little. Hopefully, not enough for her to see.

In all the Mickey Spillane books I had ever read, not once did anybody ever engage in a conversation like this.

"Don't you think it would have been nice of you to ask that question before you started groping me?" said Sunny, who was now lying with her head propped up by her elbow. "It is my body, you know."

I took a deep breath. I was starting to wish I hadn't answered the phone. Then I opened my eyes and stared very hard at the ceiling in her apartment.

"I know it's your body. You have a beautiful body, that's why I'm trying to grope it, as you put it. Are you surprised that I'm trying to do this?"

We were talking in a very casual tone, albeit a bit strained, but so far, everything was remaining pretty calm and cool.

"No. I'm not surprised. I'm quite happy about it, actually. I've been looking forward to this myself. But it would be nice if, instead of trying to break my spinal cord in half, you would say something to me like, 'Sunny, I think it's time we took our relationship to the next level. How do you feel about that?' or, 'Would you mind taking your bra off?' or, 'Sunny, I want to feel more of you than I have so far. I want to feel your breasts.'"

I could feel my face go red as soon as she said the word "breasts." My breath started coming in short bursts. I closed my eyes again. So far, in my life, the only breasts I had ever felt were the skinless, boneless chicken breasts Mom brought home from the grocery store every other Thursday night. It was my job to separate them all and put them in the freezer.

"Would it have been so hard for you to say that?" said Sunny.

I opened my eyes. If I lived to be a million years old, I could not imagine myself saying what she had just said. I could not even imagine anyone I know or have ever met for even just a minute saying anything like that.

"No, it wouldn't have been," I said anyway.

"Would you mind saying it now?" said Sunny.

I took another deep breath. By now, of course, I couldn't have cared less if her entire body was wrapped in fifty feet of black hockey tape, but I knew that a certain amount of my future was at stake, so I said, "Okay. Alright. Sunny, I would like to take your breasts to the next level."

I never finished after that. Sunny burst out laughing and so did I, although my laughter was more out of embarrassment, I had messed up the sentence so badly.

Sunny started snorting she was laughing so hard. Then she fell off the couch. I leaned over to pick her up, and then I had a better idea and started tickling her under her arms. She started squealing and fighting and kicking her feet at me. I pulled her back onto the couch and we were thrashing away at each other, me trying to tickle her some more and her trying to protect herself by clobbering me.

Then I heard a door swing open and bash against a wall. From out of nowhere Mickey appeared in the living room wearing his pajama bottoms and no top. He was holding a baseball bat in his hands. His eyes were flashing.

"Get your hands off her!" he started screaming. "Get your hands off her! That's my sister! That's my sister! Get your hands off her!"

Sunny and I both froze at once and stared at him. He was shaking, he was so mad. His big brown eyes were burning a hole right through me.

I was immediately terrified that he was going to bat me over the head.

Then Sunny exploded into laughter again, only this time, she was hysterical. She started snorting and laughing uncontrollably. She covered her mouth with one hand and pointed at Mickey with the other. Not at any particular part of him, but at him in general, and it was then that I realized he looked pretty funny, and that this whole situation was pretty funny.

So, I started laughing, but not as hard as her because Mickey had moved towards the couch and was starting to take little chops at me with his bat. He couldn't just swing away because Sunny was still on top of me, which was a good thing. He was very, very upset. For all I knew, he thought Sunny was crying instead of laughing.

"Get off him, Sunny! Get off him! Call the police! 911! 911! Help!"

After about ten minutes, we got things settled down. Sunny finally stopped laughing, although she still broke into fits, and Mickey stopped taking pokes at me.

"Just look at her," I kept trying to say to him. "Look at her. She's killing herself laughing. How can you think I was doing anything bad when she's killing herself laughing?"

"You keep your hands off my sister," he kept saying. You could tell he had just woken up, and was having a hard time figuring out what was going on.

All I could think was, thank goodness I was so lousy at doing what I was trying to do, or else we really would have had a problem to deal with.

Then he looked at Sunny and said, "I'm telling Mom. I'm telling her everything that happened."

Sunny took a break from wiping the tears from her eyes for about the tenth time and said, "Go ahead. She already knows all about what we're doing. I talked about it with her last week. What are you doing home, anyway?"

I looked at Sunny.

"You talked to your mom?" I said, before Mickey could say anything.

"I couldn't get to sleep last night so I stayed up late and watched a movie. Dad told me to take the day off. So, this morning I slept in. I woke up and I heard Harper attacking you in the living room."

"He wasn't attacking me," said Sunny, starting to giggle again. "We were play-fighting." Then she looked at me. "Although you were trying to paw me."

"You told your mom about this?" I said. This was really getting wild.

"Of course," said Sunny. "I told her how I was feeling about you and how I thought you were feeling about me. She was very happy. And, she told me to be careful. She said if things started getting out of hand or going places I didn't want them to go, to scream like crazy and grab the inside of your thigh and squeeze until you passed out. She said she learned that in a self-defense class. I'm taking one with her next time."

"The inside of my thigh?" I said.

"Assuming your pants are off," said Sunny. She was quite serious now. "Men usually protect their 'groin area,' as Mom calls it, so you grab their thigh instead."

"I'm taking that class, too," said Mickey, still holding his bat. He was so skinny. I mean, I'm not exactly a weight-lifter myself, but next to Mickey, I almost looked like one.

"The two of you should do very well at it," I said.

Sunny started to laugh again.

I looked at Mickey. He was looking at Sunny. I thought to myself, what a brave thing to do, running out here with a baseball bat, ready to defend his sister. I mean, what if I had been attacking Sunny? Or what if someone else had been? That would have been pretty scary, and there was Mickey, skinny little Mickey who looked like he weighed about ten pounds more than the bat in his hands, ready to go to battle.

Then I remembered once again how much I enjoyed Mickey's company, and that I still hadn't given him a call since coming home from camp.

"Is there a Trappers game today, Mickey?" I said. The Edmonton Trappers were the baseball team in town. I had seen them play once in my life, when Dad got free tickets, but I knew Mickey liked going to their games. He loved baseball.

He looked at me. For a moment, I wasn't sure if he still liked me or not, or trusted me. Then he said, "There's a double-header starting this afternoon."

"Well, come on," I said. "Let's go to it. My treat. I'll buy you a hot dog, too. Fatten you up a bit."

"What about me?" said Sunny. We were sitting beside each other on the couch.

I turned and looked at her. She was smiling, and looking into my eyes.

"You're too much trouble," I said. "I'll probably end up getting chased around the outfield by some guy you yell something at."

She gave me a shot in the ribs with her elbow. Then she tried to tickle me.

"Alright," I said. We were starting to wrestle again on the couch. "You can come. You can come. But be good."

She dug her fingers into my ribs.

"I'm not gonna be good," she said.

I was starting to giggle.

"Alright. Be whatever you want to be. But sit on the other side of the bleachers."

Mickey ran back into his room to get dressed.

Sunny and I fumbled around with each other, then we laid back down on the couch, with her on top of me, and kissed.

Then she asked me if everything was okay.

I nodded and said, "I think so. I'll have to talk it over with the shrink I've started seeing."

In truth, I was having the happiest time of my life.

"Is it a man shrink or a woman shrink?" said Sunny, as if it mattered.

"Both," I said. "Just one wasn't enough for me. They had to team up."

Sunny and I looked into each other's eyes again and giggled. Then Mickey came out of his bedroom and we all trooped off to the ballpark.

< 16 >

A short time later, at the end of July, Sunny received a letter from her Auntie Babs in Toronto. The letter said, straight out, "So, are you coming down here in the fall or not?"

Sunny showed it to me.

I didn't even want to see it, but I read it anyway. Her aunt was laying it on pretty heavy that Sunny should go down there.

"What do you think of all this?" I said, referring to "the bedroom all to yourself," the "unlimited fresh coffee and bagels," the "opportunity to make wonderful connections in the art world," and of course, "all of Toronto at your very doorstep," as if that was a big deal.

"How lonely is this woman?" I added. I mean, that's what it was all sounding like to me, that good old Auntie Babs just wanted some company.

"She's not lonely," said Sunny, staring at the letter. "Or maybe she is. But she's doing an awful lot of this for me, not for herself. She wants me to be an artist. She never had any kids of her own. So, she's doing what she can to help me out. She's told the same thing to Mickey. 'Find your niche and let me know about it.' She's very generous that way. Even my mom admits that."

That ended our conversation about the letter, even though I couldn't stop thinking about it.

Three days later, on a sunny Saturday afternoon, Sunny's Auntie Mavis died. She died in her home, in her own bed, with a few friends and family members around her. I guess they had all been told that the end was likely coming pretty quickly.

Sunny's mom and dad were there and they called Sunny and Mickey soon after it happened. The two of them went over to the house.

Sunny waited until she was back in her apartment before she called me. She was crying over the phone, saying that she had known for the past six months that this day was going to come, and that she thought she had been ready for it, but now that it was here, she couldn't believe it had actually finally happened.

"She always talked about this eternal life thing and going to live in a paradise where there was no pain and no fear and no anger. I used to tease her and say, 'Yes, but Auntie, there's no cigarettes there, either.' She'd just look at me and say, 'That's because no one's found a way to sneak them in yet.' But that was always her side of things, you know. I was always talking to her about where she was going and what she'd be doing. We never talked about me or Mickey down here. How we'd feel or what we'd do when she finally died."

Of course, I had no idea what to say to that.

"So, what are you doing?" I said, as compassionately as I could. That was all I could come up with. A question. And not a very good one at that.

"I'm watching a Raffi video," said Sunny.

"A what?"

"A Raffi video. *Raffi on Broadway*. He's a singer. For kids. It was my aunt's favorite. I don't know how it ended up here, but whenever she came over she'd ask to watch it. She'd just sit on the couch and listen to every song. I'm watching that. I'm waiting for "This Little Light of Mine" to come on. It's gonna kill me. She used to love that song. She used to sing it all the time."

We were quiet for a minute, then I said, "Do you want some company?"

I meant company for her as well as for me. I had really enjoyed my visit with her aunt, and I think she liked me, too. I mean, the last thing she ever said to me was, "Let's do this again sometime." I could even remember how she looked when she said it, and the way her voice sounded.

Sunny went quiet for a minute, as if she was thinking, but I'm not sure if she was thinking about my question, or how she was going to put her answer.

"Not really," she finally said. "I'm sorry, Harper. I'm just a wreck right now. We all are. It's like someone was just hit by a car. But I'll be better. I'll give you a call in a day or two. I'll let you know. You can come to the funeral if you want."

"Sure," I said, as positively as I could.

I felt a little twinge inside when she told me not to come over. All along, I had kind of seen myself as her support through all of this, which I know sounds kind of funny, since I'm not exactly a Man of Steel, but to hear that she didn't even want me around … that was a bit of a surprise.

"When is it?" I added.

"Probably near the end of the week. I'll let you know."

It wasn't until Thursday night that she phoned me again. I asked her how she was doing and she said better, now that the funeral was over.

I guess she had forgotten that I wanted to go.

She sounded very far away, and I don't mean the way a person sounds when they're calling from a car phone, or when they're talking on one of those speaker phones that makes them sound like they're sitting at the bottom of a well. I just mean she sounded far away, like her mind was far away.

Then she really dropped the bomb.

She told me she was leaving for Toronto in the morning for a visit with her Auntie Babs. She said she'd give me a call when she got back.

I couldn't believe what I was hearing. I think I was more in shock about this than I was when I heard her aunt had died.

"I know it's a surprise, Harper, but you have to believe me. I'm not going there to live. I don't think so, anyway. I'm just going for a visit. It's my mom and dad's idea. I'm a mess here. I can't sleep. I can't eat. I have to deal with this."

"How is living with your Auntie Babs going to help? I thought you didn't even like her," I said. I was mad when I said it. You could tell in my voice. But these were things I had thought about asking her a long time ago, I just didn't have the nerve to. Now, all of a sudden, I did. Now, all of a sudden, I felt like I was fighting for my life.

"Don't question me on this, Harper. I can't handle that right now. That's why I didn't ask you to the funeral. I know it sounds mean and it probably was mean, but I didn't want to be there thinking about how you were doing or if you were okay. I just wanted to be there for me and my aunt. Those were the only two people I wanted to think about and it's still that way. My Auntie Babs said I could stay with her. I have to go down there anyway to check out this school she's talking about. This way, I'll get both done at once."

"What about Mickey?" I said.

"What about Mickey?"

"Is he going, too?" I don't know what I was getting at with this question, if I was actually concerned about how he was doing, or just wondering about who was all going to Toronto, or what.

"He's dealing with it in his way. I'm dealing with it in mine," said Sunny. "He's in his room."

"Alright," I said, after a pause. I don't know what I said that for, either. It's not like she needed clearance from me to visit her aunt.

"I'll call you when I get home, okay?" she said.

I think she could tell that there wasn't much point staying on the phone, even though, for some reason, I wanted to.

"Sure," I said. "Whatever."

Then we hung up.

< 17 >

I didn't talk to Sunny again for seven days.

I went for walks with Herbie and took the bus into the city. I went to all of the places that Sunny and I had been to, not because I missed her or was feeling nostalgic about all the fun we'd had together, but because they were places that I enjoyed going to. Or so I told myself.

But really, I missed her like crazy. It was like she had already made her decision and was gone for good, or for a whole year or whatever it was. It felt like she was gone for good.

After about the third day Mom asked me what the problem was, and I said to her, "What problem?" and left it at that. I didn't feel like telling her anything more. I was quite content to walk around with all these thoughts in my head about poor me being shut out from Sunny's aunt's funeral. About people at the funeral saying, "Hey, where's Harper? I'm surprised he's not here." And other people saying, "Did you see how well he got along with Mavis?

They must have talked for hours. He was all she talked about the whole next day."

I thought about what Sunny's parents might be thinking. Were they wondering how I was doing, and wishing things had been handled a bit differently?

Mickey even called me one night and asked if I wanted to go out someplace, to a ballgame or a movie, and I said no. I told him I had some work to do, but really, I just didn't feel like doing anything that might end up being fun, although he didn't exactly sound like a barrel of laughs waiting to happen either.

It was quite the load I was carrying, and I surprised myself by packing it around for almost the entire week because, as I said, I am not exactly a body-builder when it comes to lifting or carrying things.

Then one night I was out with Herbie at a little park near our house watching this family playing at the playground and I thought again about Sunny's Auntie Mavis. But this time, it was different.

I thought about the little conversation we had shared together and how comfortable I had felt with her. She had talked to me and listened to what I was saying. She had called me a writer, not a kid who wanted to be a writer. Or a kid who was a dreamer. I know lots of people her age who roll their eyes and shake their heads when kids say they want to be writers or actors or singers.

Most of Mom and Dad's friends think I'm just floating along on a raft on some ocean somewhere, living the comfortable life of an only-child-at-home-with-rich-parents. I've told a few of them that I would like to be a writer and they just smile politely and take another sip of their drink.

One of them, a friend of Mom's named Mrs. Von Heighten, said to me once, "Surely you need a degree for that," because she knows that Mom's Big Fear for me school-wise is that I won't go to university after I graduate from high school, and Mom has never been one to keep her Big Fears to herself.

I said, "I don't know if they hand out Writers' Degrees at university or not these days," which drew an electrified stare from everyone who heard me.

But Sunny's Auntie Mavis never judged me for a second. She heard that I was interested in writing so she called me a writer, just like that. And she talked to me as if I was a writer, even though I didn't have a clue what she was talking about.

Then I thought, no wonder Sunny was so devastated by her aunt's death. What a great person she must have been to have around. What conversations they must have had.

Then I started thinking a little differently about Sunny. I saw her as someone who had just lost her very best friend. Not a relative she saw at Christmas and Easter or an aunt she had actually been sort of close with, but her very best friend, because really, that's what her Auntie Mavis was to her. And Sunny, like myself, didn't seem to have many friends. Or if she did, she sure didn't talk about them very much. She never said things to me like, "Oh, come to this party, Harper. All my friends will be there. I can't wait for you to meet them." Or she never said, "My girlfriend met her boyfriend at a camp, too. Can you believe that? My best friend in the whole world and she met her boyfriend the same way I met you."

She never said anything like that.

But she told her aunt everything and they seemed to enjoy each other's company so much. Then all of a sudden her aunt died, and I got upset because Sunny didn't want me around for a few days.

"It's a terrible thing," said Mom, after I finally told her and Dad what was going on. I pretty well had to share it with somebody. "You think you're ready for it, but you're not. You're never ready for it. You fool yourself."

"Sunny said it felt like someone had been hit by a car," I said.

"That's how it can feel sometimes," said Dad, the Doctor.

We were all just hanging around the living room talking about it. Dad was sitting in his chair going through the newspaper. Mom was having a coffee on the couch. I was just standing in the doorway of the living room.

"I've been around plenty of people who thought they had a hold on things, only to see them fall completely apart when the end finally came. It can be a very difficult time. Especially if they've never gone through it before. Some people want to be alone. Some can't be alone," he said.

"Well," said Mom, taking a sip of her coffee, "for now, let's just hope Sunny and her family get what they need to get over this, whether it's company or solitude or whatever. Then they can all get back together and deal with this other thing."

She looked over at me. Then she said, "Isn't that what all this sulking around for the past week has really been about, whether Sunny will go to Toronto or not? To this art school?"

I didn't say anything. She was right, of course, but I still didn't say anything. I just looked at her. Then I looked down at the floor. Where else are you supposed to look when someone has you like that?

"I think it is," said Mom, moving right along. She was even nodding her head when she said it. "And if you don't mind me saying, Harper, I think it's a bit selfish of you to not be encouraging her to go, especially at a time like this. She has a dream to be an artist and an opportunity to immerse herself almost completely in it for one whole year, and right smack in the middle of her way is you. Not just you, she has family here and all that, I heard her the other night, I know where her mother is coming from, but for Sunny right now, you are a major obstacle. And only you can help her get around it."

I felt like clapping when she was finished. She was so motivational. And not once did she look down at her notes.

Then Dad cleared his throat and started to talk. I guess it was time for another *Chicken-Soup-for-the-Soul*-story, or whatever those charming little things are called that half my teachers at school keep reading to us.

"You know, Harper, when I was high school,

there was a girl I knew who wanted to be a singer. She was singing all the time. She sent demo tapes to every recording studio in North America. Then one day, she got a call. Someone in New York wanted her to audition for them, or record with them, or whatever. So she went down there and she fell flat on her face. She didn't put two notes together that made any sense. She said she was awful. So she came back and now she's a teacher. Right here in Emville. I saw her a few years ago and she told me her story. I asked her what happened. She had a beautiful voice and she could stand up anywhere and belt out a song. She told me that she never had any encouragement from home to make it as a real singer. Her mom and dad were terrified of her going down there alone, but they couldn't afford to go with her. Or they chose not to. I don't know. But she got down there and she was all by herself, and scared out of her mind, and she started believing everything her parents had told her about, 'You're never gonna make it,' and 'Those people in the music business are vultures,' and 'You're gonna be killed if you go down there.' She said as soon as she stepped off the plane, all she wanted to do was come home. And when she got home, she couldn't wait to leave again. And she did. She left and she never came back. Then over time, both her parents passed away, and her brothers and sisters moved on, so then she moved back.

"You don't want that to happen to Sunny. You don't want her to go down there and start missing you and feeling badly because you're all sad and angry over here. That's no way to be when you're trying to study. You want her to excel. You want her to come back brimming with confidence, and the two of you will have a wonderful life together."

I stood there and waited for him to finish. I felt so fortunate that Mom and Dad knew what I wanted even before I did. It really saved me the aggravation of trying to figure it out on my own.

"It's only for a year," said Mom, for reinforcement. "Remember that. You're friends with her brother. You and Mickey can chum around together. And who knows? Maybe we can fly you down there at Christmas or Spring Break, if you're doing well at school, of course. That can be your present. A trip to Toronto. Wouldn't that be exciting? You and Sunny wandering around together in that big city. I'd have to go with you, of course. I couldn't bear to leave you alone."

I gave her a look.

That did sound fun, actually. Taking a trip down there to see her. And I knew everything they were saying made sense. But you know what? I still wanted her to stay. I really did. Sunny wasn't going to fall apart and quit art and become a teacher just because she missed out on one year at an art school.

"I'll tell you something else," said Mom, who seemed to be talking nonstop lately. "Just between the three of us – if her father's a librarian and her mother's an unpublished writer, they're not going to have the money to send her to this school. Even with free room and board, they're not going to be able to afford that."

Dad looked at her and thought for a moment and nodded.

I looked at both of them. Inside, I could feel a wonderful, burning glow. Mom was right. Of course, they couldn't afford it. I felt a big smile coming on.

Then I felt sick. What a crummy thing to say, and what an even crummier thing to get excited about. *I get to stay with my girlfriend because her parents are too poor to send her to a school.*

"Maybe they do, maybe they don't," I said, turning to leave the room. It was the best I could come up with, and I really didn't want to be there anymore.

"If they do, I'd be very surprised," said Mom, sounding supremely confident.

For a minute there, I actually hoped Sunny would surprise her.

< 18 >

Sunny phoned me two days later. She was home again and sounding much, much better. She said she'd had a wonderful time and that she wanted to talk to me about a few things. In person.

I hopped on a bus in about three seconds and rode into the city.

I got to her apartment and she opened the door and gave me a great big hug. You don't know how good that hug felt. Or maybe you do, so you know it's too hard to describe, other than to say that I actually closed my eyes and forgot where I was until it was over.

When we stood back and looked at each other, Sunny had a tear in her eye, and she was sniffing.

That's when I knew she was going back to Toronto. I don't know how I knew, but I did. I just had a feeling.

"Let's go for a walk," she said, closing the door behind her.

I couldn't move. I felt sick to my stomach. I

thought I was going to cry.

"Come on," she said.

"Are you going back to Toronto?" I said. I had to know, even though I did know.

She looked right at me and smiled. Then her eyes really filled up and we just stood there in the hallway and hugged each other.

We didn't say a word to each other until we got outside. I couldn't even say anything then.

"My Auntie Mavis gave me some money to go," said Sunny, finally. "She said she thought it would be good for me. That I'd learn a lot and meet some people who could give me some good advice."

I was going to say something like, "They don't have people around here who can do that?" But I didn't. There was no way Sunny was going to go against something her Auntie Mavis said.

"You know what else she said? She said she thought you were the kind of person who would understand, that you would appreciate what this meant to me."

Sunny was looking at me when she said that. I guess she was waiting for a reaction.

This was a tough one to react to.

"When did she tell you all this?" I said. I had to buy some time. Besides, it did make me feel good to hear that, that her aunt thought I was somebody who would understand all of this. But what I liked most was Sunny talking about coming back to me. I did not want this to be a goodbye for good.

"We had a talk the day after she met you. My parents told me about the money last night. They wanted to see if I liked it down there or not, which I did. I mean, I like it here, too, but for one year, I could handle it down there. Auntie Babs has even set aside some studio space for me in her apartment. It's huge in there. I never realized that before."

"It'll be tough for you to be in a school again," I said, as a reminder that she was a product of home schooling, although I doubt she had forgotten.

"I know," said Sunny, "but this school is different, and I've met some of the instructors and they all seem nice. They liked my work. They said I shouldn't have any problem, as long as I work hard enough. I told them my boyfriend lives in Alberta, so I'll have nothing to do there but eat, sleep, and paint. They were quite happy to hear that."

We walked on for a while. She was going, there was no question about that, and her enthusiasm was starting to rub off on me, a little. I mean, that did sound almost perfect: a school where pretty well all you do is study art; her own studio; and, no distractions from her meddling, pawing, groping boyfriend.

I started telling her about my conversation the night before with Mom and Dad (except the part about the money). She asked me what I thought about being supportive and encouraging and everything.

I started to say something like, "Well, we all need encouragement and support," or something dumb like that, but then I felt a lump the size of a baseball well up in my throat. I didn't want to be supportive of her when she was down there in Toronto. I didn't want to be a good boy, or whatever her Auntie Mavis had called me. I wanted to be a little twerp and say to Sunny, "If you go, it's goodbye, baby. I'm not waiting for nobody. It's me, or art."

"They also said they'd fly me down to see you sometime. Probably at Christmas. Maybe I could even go twice," I said, by way of an answer. I didn't know what I was thinking about.

Sunny looked at me. Her eyes were so excited.

"They said that?" she said.

"Mom did," I said. "And her hand is a lot closer to the money than Dad's is."

"They said they'd fly you down twice?"

"Well, I said that. But what the heck? They have enough flight points to orbit the earth for a month. They could buy me a couple of tickets."

"So, you could come see me twice, and I could come back here at least once. That's three times we'll see each other for, like, a full week at a time. That's fantastic!" Sunny actually seemed genuinely excited with all this.

I started to get a little excited again myself. It would be fun to go and see her. Not quite as enjoyable as seeing her every day right here at home, but it would be alright.

"I can pal around with Mickey until you get back. I'll introduce him to my friend, Billy. I think the two of them will hit it off. We could have some fun together."

"While I'm slaving away learning how to draw," said Sunny.

We looked at each other. She was smiling. She still had tears in her eyes, but they were pretty well gone.

I don't know what my eyes looked like. Inside, I felt lousy – a kind of empty feeling. But I also knew there was no way Sunny was going to disappear from my life just because she was going away for a while.

At least, I sure didn't think that was going to happen.

"We'll be okay, Harper," she said.

"I know," I said, even though I didn't. How would I know that for sure? I'd never been through anything like this before. I did like saying it, though.

"You want to get something to eat?" she said, a minute or so later.

"I'd rather roll around in the grass," I said, looking at her. She looked so beautiful again. "I can eat when you're gone."

She liked that idea, so we walked down towards the park.

I wasn't feeling completely awful anymore, but I was sure looking forward to the end of next year.

A Beautiful Place on Yonge Street is the third
installment in the adventures of Harper Winslow.
The Tuesday Cafe won the R. Ross Annett Award
for Children's Literature and made the ALA's
"Popular Paperbacks" list for 1998. *A Fly Named
Alfred* was short-listed for the prestigious Mr.
Christie Book Award.